I0456327

A Wolf in Patchwork Clothing

A Novella of the Patchwork History

Travis Coleman

DEDICATION

To my wife who lets me pursue writing.
To my co-workers for all the little ideas you give me.
Finally, to all those who have read this and helped on the edits.
I couldn't have done it without you.

ISBN: 0692632336
ISBN-13:978-0692632338

ACKNOWLEDGMENTS

Cover design by
The Cover Collection

Originally posted at
http://travcoleman.blogspot.com/

CONTENTS

CHAPTER 1

Torchlight flickered off Patch's skin as he stood on the gallows. The feel of the heavy hempen rope against his neck irritated his skin, but he knew that he couldn't get everything he wanted. This was just one of those parts of his life that he had no control over.

Perhaps it was time for him to move on, to go somewhere a bit more civilized. He hadn't been to California yet, but from everything he had heard it was a golden land. Although the last Gold Rush back in '49 hadn't lasted very long, it had been almost forty years which meant almost anything could have happened. He could also go back east, he hadn't been east of the Mississippi River since the end of the Civil War.

"Patrick, you have been accused of killing Deputy Smith, we have a witness that says she saw you do it." The sheriff began as he stepped up on to the scaffolding. They had built it this afternoon and Patch hoped it would collapse under the extra weight. Around him the townsfolk were gathered around to watch the proceedings.

"Then why haven't you pulled that lever there James? You afraid that the towns people will string you up next? Afraid they'll call you a murderer too?" Patch asked. He looked out and could see the betrothed of the deputy among the crowd. Her father was trying to comfort her but the tears continued to fall.

"Shut up! Do you have anything to say in your defense? Do you want to beg for your life?" the sheriff asked.

"Nope, it didn't work for your deputy when I pulled him off that girl. He just sat there with his pants around his ankles crying out, 'please don't hurt me'. But to do that to a girl who was only thirteen is the worst kind of coward. He didn't deserve to live."

"That's my Deputy and friend you're talking about!" the sheriff snapped.

"I don't care if he was the President, he was a coward, a yellow-bellied coward," Patch let the last few words stretch as he spoke them. Until the sudden hurried movement of the sheriff towards the handle cut him off.

"That may have been the case, but you aren't the law here. I am the law, and your sentence is to hang by the neck until..."

A blast from a shotgun cut him off, causing the entire crowd to jump. Several people began to examine themselves to be sure they hadn't been shot. When they turned to see where the shot had come from, the sheriff dove behind the upright of the gallows.

"Sheriff, that man doesn't deserve to die," came a voice from the crowd. The woman's voice was strong, carrying over the crowd and their assorted cries. "That man kept one of my girls from being violated by a lawman. Why should anyone in this town trust you?"

Patch smiled at Sally, she had a backbone. She needed one to survive in this territory and to run the business she did. This area had long been home to bandit raids on homesteads, yet she had weathered it for years. Now seeing her stand up to the sheriff made him proud of her.

Around the gallows the crowd was scattering, a path opening between Sally and Patch. Patch saw motion to his side and glanced at the lever. The last thing that he wanted was to have his feet dropped out from under him prematurely. He felt himself sigh as he realized it was just the Sheriff stepping out from behind the gallows pole.

"You know Sally, discharging a weapon in town is enough to get you locked up in a cell tonight. It'd be a shame to have to arrest you for disrupting the peace," the sheriff grinned. "I see your horse tied up over there in front of the general store. Get on that horse, ride out of town, and let the law handle this. I'll not be asking so nicely next time."

Sally hesitated, looking back towards where her horse was tied. He could see the horse stamping it's hoof nervously due to the gunfire. This was a development that Patch hadn't foreseen when the sheriff had hauled him in. Right now he was supposed to be dangling from a rope, not in the middle of a fight where bullets might fly at any moment.

Again movement out of the corner of his eye caused him to focus on the sheriff. His hand had moved towards the gun holster at his side, and it looked like he was going to draw.

"Sally!" Patch called out, hoping that she would notice before he drew and shot her in the back. This cemented his opinion, the lawmen of this town were cowards to a man. What they really needed was someone with a backbone to run this place. But Sheriff Roberts was only interested in one thing, how comfortable he could make his life.

Sally cranked the lever on her shotgun, forcing another shell into the chamber as she looked back to the gallows. It was one of those new designs, and it had cost her quite a bit, but the time saved on reloading had scared away bandits more than once in the last year.

The sheriff's hand moved away from the gun and fell to his side as she began to speak. "Sheriff, how about you let me take care of my own. I'm far enough out of this town that you send him back with me and you'll never hear from him again. I'll make sure of it, and you can go back to skimming money off my sales like you always have."

Everyone watching could see the sheriff's gaze harden at the mention of skimming. Anyone who had been in the saloon with him had heard the explanation more than once. It wasn't stealing because the law needed to be taken care of. They were only as safe as their lawman was well fed and, based on the girth the man was beginning to attain, he was well looked after.

"I can't do that Miss Sally. I understand the claim that one of your girls was involved and on your property. You have to understand he was a well respected man of the community, so justice needs to be served."

Her laugh cut through the night and left the remainder of the people watching from nearby places silent. "If that's a well respected man of this community I want nothing to do with it. That man was a pervert and was constantly trying to take advantage of my girls. These girls are orphans and have suffered enough without having a power hungry lecher stalking them."

This time it was Patch who laughed, "I couldn't have described him better myself. I think my favorite part was when I pulled my knife and he pissed himself. True, you probably couldn't tell due to the blood loss that followed, but trust me sheriff, he was yellow and this city doesn't need a coward like him defending it."

The sheriff bristled and Patch could see color in his cheeks despite the poor light. "This is why I have to hang him, if he showed some kind of remorse for his actions I would consider letting him go, but he's little more than a cold blooded killer."

"You don't know him like I do Sheriff." Sally interrupted. She had the gun lowered to the ground, which Patch felt might be a mistake. "That man has been the best herder that I could have asked for. He's killed several coyotes and kept the sheep safe. Usually you expect to lose a couple, but he's kept the flock alive and thriving through the summer."

"I don't see how this comes into play. This isn't a discussion about whether he is good at his job. This is about one thing, plain and simple; murder." Patch watched as the sheriff began to pace back and forth. This was getting him nowhere and he was getting bored.

It was true enough that he had done a good job at being a shepherd, but that was because it gave him a chance to do whatever he liked and still eat. The less supervision he had, the better he seemed to do. The feelings from Sally though were something he hadn't expected at all.

She had always been good to him, though he knew that this was going to be his last season working with her. He also knew something that she didn't, something that no one had noticed, he'd ripped out the deputy's tongue. Sure it was a coward's tongue, but his was going rotten. The flavor of each bite of food, each drink of water, had been tinged with that sickly taste of rancid meat. He was even beginning to smell it in his nostrils with each breath. The deputy's little display had come along at just the right time. If the girl hadn't fainted at the sight of blood she would have probably died after the deputy.

That was what made the whole thing ridiculous, he had been ready to leave town after ripping the man's tongue out. Instead he had decided to take the girl back to the house and explain what had happened. Somehow Sally had convinced him that the sheriff would be understanding. Now he stood on the gallows and was getting sick of all of the talk. Something needed to happen, one of them needed to shoot one another. That, or maybe the sheriff would show he wasn't a coward and would pull the lever.

"So, what you're saying is that if you shoot a man who is breaking the law it's justice, yet if someone else does it, that's murder." Sally spat back at the sheriff. "I don't remember how you became sheriff."

"I took over for my father who served as sheriff for years. He taught me what's right and what's wrong."

"So we're not an American territory anymore? We're living in a monarchy now?" Sally broke in. Patch watched as she brought the shotgun back up towards the gallows. "Should I be addressing you as your majesty?"

"You're not making any sense. This is just the way things go around here. You're the first person who has had a problem with my decisions."

"Both of you shut up!" Patch shouted. Sally and the sheriff looked at him as though they had forgotten he was present. "Sally, I killed him so I'll get punished. Sheriff, you're a coward just like your deputy. If all it takes is one person with a shotgun to make you question your justice this place will be overrun."

"That isn't..." the sheriff began, but Patch was done listening.

"You're going to hang me? When? You're too busy flapping your gums to do it. So I guess I'll just have to take justice into my own hands again." With this he jumped towards the lever, kicking it and releasing the trap door.

The rope fell taut, not breaking his neck, and he began to laugh. It echoed through the night and he could see both the sheriff and Sally's eyes widen. Their jaws dropped and cries began to come from several of the nearby buildings. That just made the whole thing more amusing, and his laughter continued.

"Sheriff, make it stop!" came a shout from a nearby building where a child was crying. Patch continued to laugh, his eyes tearing up with amusement at the way they acted.

His breath began to wane, the rope making it so he couldn't continue the laughing with any volume. Still his chest bounced and the rope shook with his mirth. That was when he heard the gunshot and felt the sudden warmth in his chest.

He began to bleed feeling his delight ebbing out of him. As the blood began to fill his boots Patch felt his consciousness fading. The last thing he remembered was someone muttering a prayer underneath their breath.

CHAPTER 2

Sally stepped from the barn after leaving her horse eating quietly in its stable. She knew that if she had roused them, one of the farm hands would have been willing to come out here and take care of her. But as she had brushed Sage, her paint mare, it had given her time to ponder what had happened in the square.

The scene played itself through her mind, and a part of her wished she hadn't fired the warning shot. If she'd just taken aim at the Sheriff with her shotgun and pulled the trigger, it probably would have made her argument more effective. What about the consequences? Could she live her life as a fugitive? It would have left her girls, which she fought so hard to protect, to be thrown to the wolves.

A chill ran through her spine an image of perverts like that deputy circling the house like vultures, came to her mind. Without realizing it, she clutched the shotgun a little tighter and double-checked that it was loaded.

She stepped onto the porch of the small ranch home that housed the five girls she worked with, herself, and the looms. There was a bench outside and she took a moment to kick any extra mud and dirt from her boots there. As she looked up, she noticed a tin plate tucked underneath the edge of a bench. The sight of it sitting there derailed her mind from the gallows scene earlier, and from the gunshot which had left Patch dripping blood like a cider press.

Those farm hands, the two she had left, didn't seem to understand the importance of getting the dishes washed at night. Did they not want to use clean plates? Did they like their morning eggs covered in dust and licked by whatever critter happened to amble through?

Shrugging, she picked it up and opened the door, seeing a burning lantern waiting for her on a hook inside the door. She appreciated the sentiment. Appreciated the fact that the girls would leave a lamp burning for her. What she didn't appreciate were the two men sitting in the rockers by the spinning wheels. One of them had their feet up on the base, wedged between the wheel and the bobbin. A part of her wanted to raise the shotgun and fire off a shot to wake the two of them up. Yet thinking of the girls upstairs, especially Emma who had been the subject of the deputy's advances, stayed her finger on the trigger.

Instead she sat on the stairs and unloaded the gun, removing each cartridge and placing them in the pocket of her apron hanging on the banister. She'd find a proper place for them in the morning, for now she just wanted to get some sleep.

The thud of the stock on the floor as she set the gun down startled one of the men awake, Samuel, the man who had his feet resting on the base of the spinning wheel. He quickly unraveled himself and stood up.

"I'm sorry Miss Sally, I must have just fallen asleep," he stammered. His voice was slurred with the vestiges of sleep.

"It's okay Samuel. But if I catch you with your feet on one of my spinning wheels again, I'll scalp you and use your hair for my thread," she grinned at him and saw him flush.

"I'm so sorry, I was just trying to get comfortable and this rocker wasn't built for a guy my size."

She knew that much was true, she'd had them built to be her size and she was far from the giant that he was. Samuel towered over her and had to duck to get through the doors here. She didn't think he minded all that much though. She'd first met him at the mission that had saved her life, taking her in and giving her an education. He'd been a shepherd there too, working with the animals that provided the mission with the vital food and materials they needed to live. That was also where she realized the value of weaving which her mother had taught.

One of the sisters there had been working on weaving a blanket when Sally had arrived and corrected her. It a short time Sally was leading many of the sisters in preparing looms the way she had been taught. While they rushed through their work, she took her time. Her first full blanket had taken a year. The priest in charge of the mission had been amazed at the quality of the work, and the price it had fetched had provided for assistance with many of the orphans that they had taken in.

That was where she had started, and instead of taking vows she decided to take in orphans from the mission and teach them the trade. Samuel had followed her from there, bringing his small flock which had now grown, as had their entire farm.

"You know Miss Sally, I don't know why you're so concerned. If I had been anyone thinking of causing trouble down here the thought of the deputy's body would have made me think twice," he said. "I don't like how he did it, but Patrick may have done us a world of good with his actions."

She only nodded, but she still didn't like leaving the girls unguarded. Sadly next summer, when the flocks went out to pasture in the hills again, she'd have to figure out some other form of protection. Considering her dealings with Sheriff Roberts, she didn't know if she could wait even that long. That man always was looking for a way to take a little bit more, it was only a matter of time before he came for her farm.

"Do you want me to go out and walk the grounds now Miss Sally?" Samuel asked. This derailed her train of thought and she was surprised that she had forgotten he was standing there. Something about Samuel made him almost fade into the background.

Sally had always seen Samuel as a follower, never a leader. He never seemed to speak his mind or have any sort of original idea of his own but he was valuable in other ways. He knew how to raise, birth, and shear the sheep. He seemed like an agricultural god at times, planting and fertilizing in the spring to keep the garden crops alive through the summer. There always seemed to be extras once everything was preserved. She just wished he was someone she could talk to, someone who attracted her attention the way Patrick had.

There was something about Patrick that gave him a presence. When she'd first seen him she'd had chills run up her spine. He had a way with words which had reassured her, and even Samuel had accepted him rather quickly.

Now he was gone, just another person in her life that had left her. The only person who hadn't left her was Samuel. She wondered, and not for the first time, if he should have been born a dog. He would have been great big beastly thing which could easily be alpha, but did he have the backbone?

Perhaps that was why she'd found herself so attracted to Patrick. He'd had a backbone, he wasn't going to sit around and wait for someone else to decide what to do. The man would have been the leader in a pack.

"Samuel, just go get some sleep. We'll worry about things in the morning. Perhaps then I'll relate what I saw in town and everyone can help me puzzle things out from there."

"Okay, I'll get Jacob and we'll head out to our quarters," Samuel replied. She didn't give him a chance to say anything else. Instead she turned and made her way upstairs, listening as Jacob and Samuel made their way out the front door. Then she turned to the girls room. Beneath the door she could make out a sliver of light meaning at least someone was awake.

As quietly as she could, she made her way into the room, the hinges squeaking told the girl who was sitting up that someone had entered. Once the girl, Mary, saw who it was, she relaxed visibly and went back to reading the bible in her lap. Mary sat next to Emma's bed with a lamp burning as she had the last few nights.

"How's she doing? Is she having nightmares again tonight?" Sally asked. Mary only nodded, and she knew that before long she'd probably wake one of the other girls to watch over her. Sally would normally volunteer to take a shift but today had taken far too much out of her already.

"I'll take over in the morning. I just need to get some rest."

"So did they?" Mary asked. The question hung in the air between them. It was Sally's her turn to nod in answer. In the light of the lantern tears glistened on Mary's cheek. Sally knew that given a little privacy, she would probably break down too.

Still, she stood and waited to see if there were any other questions from the girl who was keeping a vigilant watch. Mary just turned back to the bible she was reading, and Sally took it as a sign that it was time to retire for the night. To go to her bed and hopefully not dream of the that single gunshot. Of the kick that ended the life of a man that she may have loved.

* * * * *

Thomas slung the body over his shoulder and motioned for his boss, Peter, to release the rope. When the weight of the body settled on him in full he staggered before catching his balance.

"Peter, get over here and take the legs of this guy. He's heavier than he looks," Thomas complained. It had been a busy day, they'd spent all day assembling the gallows and now they had to move the body to get a coffin built for him. They had the wood milled at least, it was just a matter of assembly now.

"You look like you got him. Besides, you made me carry this pole over without any help. Seems you could use some lifting to make up for it." Peter replied. He took his time coiling the rope that had been freed and then loosening the noose around Patrick's neck.

"Honestly, I'm going to kill you if you don't hurry up. That or maybe just leave you here to haul the damn body. I didn't hire on to do this."

"Look, your father arranged for you to apprentice under me. That means you get to learn the good as well as the bad. It's not all tables, chairs, and stools. In a small town like this, we're responsible for loads more."

"Where did you learn the trade then?" Thomas asked. He felt the body beginning to slide off his shoulder and scrambled to redistribute it.

"I started down in Santa Fe, then I decided I'd come up here and homestead. It's worked out well, and with talk of a rail line coming this way it couldn't be a better place to be." Peter dropped the coiled rope onto the platform before taking the other arm.

"I thought you were going to grab the feet." Thomas snapped. He had to readjust the body a third time, now it was getting frustrating.

"I ain't touching those shoes. At least not until I have to." As Peter hoisted the weight he could tell what his apprentice meant. "Yeah he is heavier than I expected. Now lets haul him away."

They fell into a rhythm as they moved down the stairs and towards their shop. Left, right, one, two, they counted quietly to themselves. That was when Thomas felt the breath on his neck which could only have come from the corpse.

"Shit!" Thomas called. He let go of the body and jumped away. Peter began to curse as well before letting go. The body collapsed to the ground.

"Why did you drop him?" Peter yelled.

"He ain't dead. He breathed on me!" Thomas called back, his eyes intent on the corpse.

"He took a bullet to the chest. You don't come back from something like that. Odds are it's just wind escaping the body." Peter scowled at him and motioned back to the corpse. "Now get over here and help me get it into the shop. We need to get this done and get him buried. If we don't the shop will smell to high hell and will take weeks to air out."

Thomas accepted that answer but still approached the body cautiously, certain that at any moment it was going to jump up and grab him. Peter motioned in the darkness for him to hurry.

"Look, if he is alive he ain't gonna be happy with us for building the gallows."

"If he is alive I'll buy you enough drinks that you'll forget the whole scene. Now pick him up." Peter's last words spurred Thomas to motion and together they lifted the corpse off the ground and carried it the rest of the way to the carpenter's shop.

CHAPTER 3

Thomas pounded a nail into the plank before wiping his brow. The heat was setting in and he would be happy to get a cover over the corpse before it began to stink. He lifted the lid and maneuvered it into place at the foot of the coffin. That was when he heard the heavy iron wheels on the back of the shop begin to roll.

"I'm telling you sheriff, the body is almost sealed up but it's those gravediggers that are lazy. You need to get them up there so I can get this out of my shop," Peter complained as he made his way through the door.

Thomas could see Sheriff Roberts now, the sunlight coming through the door gleaming off the bronze of his badge. You could insult the sheriff but you didn't tarnish the badge. Thomas had seen a man spit on the badge once at the saloon, the man was unconscious before Sheriff Roberts was pulled off him. Had it not been for several strong men in the saloon they would have built a coffin that night too.

"The gravediggers say until they have a body they aren't going to start digging. That's the problem with too many people thinking in this town. They should listen and act like my father was still in charge," Sheriff Roberts replied.

Thomas watched as they came over to the table. He was about to speak when Peter addressed him. "Why don't you have the top on already?"

"I've only just finished it. But I think I need to head down to the blacksmith and get a few more nails. We only have a few and I don't know if they'll hold."

"They'll be fine. We don't have time for that, we need to get the coffin up to the cemetery before they'll start digging." Peter said. He was lifting the lid into place as he talked. Thomas followed his lead and grabbed the few nails that they had. He counted them as they rolled across his palm, only five left.

"Gimme those nails Thomas and go get the horse harnessed. The Sheriff and I will get this loaded onto the wagon. Now hurry, I wanted this out of here hours ago."

Thomas placed the nails on the work table and headed towards the front door. As he stepped into the afternoon light he was surprised to see Samuel approaching. They all knew Samuel from playing cards in the Saloon. But why was he here? That bothered him. After everything that had happened last night this was the last place he should be. In fact, to see anyone from Sally's farm in town just seemed odd.

This was the kind of thing his parents had told him stories about. They'd moved here from Arkansas where feuds were common among families. Something as simple as a stolen goose would cause generations of fighting and distrust. All day, as he'd built the coffin, there had been thoughts of people coming in with guns to steal the body and bury it themselves. More than once he'd heard a board creaking and almost dropped his hammer.

As Samuel entered the shop Thomas was certain there would be gunshots any moment. He ran down the side of the building towards the barn. A second wall between him and the bullets would be favorable. Putting the horse between himself and the guns seemed like an even better idea.

As he entered the barn everything seemed still. There were no shots, no loud yelling, the only noise he heard was the nickering of the horse in the corral. Opening the tack room in the back, he retrieved the bit, bridle, and harness for the wagon. In the back of his head though, his thoughts wandered.

What were they talking about in there? They weren't yelling, they weren't shouting, and they weren't shooting. Sheriff Roberts hadn't come out of the shop either, which seemed odd. Thomas knew that if someone had recently executed his friend the last place he'd like to be is in the same room with the man.

The horse saw the bridle from across the corral and trotted over to him. It began nuzzling his hands looking for the carrot, apple, or whatever treat he had brought.

"Sorry Daisy, nothing for you today. But if you're good on the trip I'll get you something for dinner tonight. Maybe sneak you some extra oats." He said it fondly as he patted the horse on the nose.

The horse whickered when she wasn't given a treat, but she didn't retreat. They had a good working relationship and he was glad Daisy wasn't stubborn, like some of the others he'd seen in town.

"Here is your bridle, lass, and it looks lovely on you," he commented as he put the bit in her mouth. He didn't know why he talked to the horse like this. He'd learned it from the farrier on one of his trips to get the horse shod. The man barely said a word in setting a price, but as soon as he was with the animal he never shut up. The man insisted that it calmed the animals, made them feel more at ease, which lead to an easier job for him. For what it was worth it did make Thomas feel more at ease around her. Besides, everyone needs someone to talk to from time to time, even if that someone responds in neighs and whinnies.

Once he got the bridle fastened he walked around the horse, laying the harness on her shoulders and moving to get everything tightened.

"So you know Daisy, we're heading up to the cemetery today. On the bright side you won't have so much weight to control on the way down the hill. So come on and let's get you hooked up to the wagon."

His nerves were calm as he led the horse out of the corral. Perhaps the farrier was right about talking calming the nerves. If only he could get away with it inside the shop with Peter around. So many of his problems came from Peter and his demands.

Approaching the sliding door he heard a voice raised inside.

"I don't care how you get it done Samuel, just get it taken care of!" Shouted Sheriff Roberts. "I can't think of everything, now start acting like a man and find a solution."

Thomas froze, one hand holding the bridle, the other on the handle. What were they shouting about? He looked over his shoulder towards the corral, would it be safer there?

"Look, I'm beginning to think the deal is off James. I feel like you're not living up to your end." Samuel replied. His voice was raised and Thomas was sure it had a hint of panic in it.

"If you try to back out of this I'll hang you. The gallows are still standing and I'm sure this Patrick fellow didn't kill anyone by himself. You were there with him as Patrick slit his throat. You're a guilty party." Even through the door Thomas could hear the grin. It was a tell the Sheriff had, he always took that tone when he thought he had you beat.

"I wasn't there, I was out with the flocks and Jacob will confirm it. We were bringing the second flock out of the hills and..."

"And nothing! Like I told Miss Sally, I'm the law here and if I believe you were an accomplice then you were. So don't give me any lip and get out of here. You're not doing us any favors hanging around here."

Daisy whinnied and Thomas knew that he had been given away, cautiously, certain that a bullet may come flying at him, he pulled the door open. The three men were gathered around the casket. Peter was up on the table, hammer in hand and a nail in the side of his mouth. The other two men were standing face-to-face along the side. Samuel clung to a few scraps of cloth which Thomas knew were Patrick's personal items. They didn't bury good belts, boots, and other items that were hard to come by.

"I need to get going," Samuel said as Thomas entered the shop with the horse. Thomas acted like he hadn't heard anything, it was a personal conversation that he had no business listening to. He just wished that the whole thing hadn't felt so odd. What deal were they talking about? They often played cards down at the saloon but they never discussed deals. Was there something happening that he should know about?

"Thomas, I'm going to need your help over here to move this thing onto the wagon." Peter called to him. Thomas only nodded and continued fastening the horse to the cart.

Whispering into the horses ear as he changed sides Thomas said, "None of our business right Daisy? We just do the work around here."

The other men didn't seem to notice. They were focused on Samuel who was leaving through the front.

CHAPTER 4

A thud, followed by the skitter of dirt, brought Patch back to consciousness. His last memory had been of laughing, dangling by his neck, knowing that he'd stolen the show from that pompous Sheriff and his rules. Nothing was more annoying than a man who felt he was too important to do his duty.

Another thud spilled dirt through a knot hole in the top of the box, bringing him back to his current situation. His mental ranting and raving would need to wait a bit longer, or at least until he was able to breathe fresh air again.

Slowly he went through a mental list, figuring out what was working inside and what wasn't. He was able to inhale, but his movements seemed dulled. He could see flickering lamplight shining through the knot hole, and his mouth tasted musty and dry. It was just that one key piece inside him that was going to make things difficult.

He tried to flex his muscles and felt a bit of strength in them, though not as much as he would have liked. The wooden sides squeezed his shoulders, and he could feel the grain of it scraping against the bottoms of his feet.

"Figures. This is exactly where I didn't want to end up," he muttered.

Pulling his legs up slightly he felt his knees hit the wood of the lid. He had a few inches to work with here at least. The light flickering through the boards was getting dimmer as another thud sounded on the top of the box, reminding him he had a limited amount of time.

He slid his arms up along his belly, doing it slowly to be sure he didn't waste all of his strength. The problem of not having a working heart was you didn't have any air to replenish your strength. Once you burned through what you had it knocked you out and left you helpless. He'd spent far too much time being helpless since last night; it was time for him to move on.

Once his hands reached his shoulders, he rotated them placing the palms against the lid. Inhaling in preparation of what he was about to do, he could feel some of the goop that was his blood oozing from the hole in his chest. He had to be smart about this; slow movements, nothing sudden or quick. He started to press the lid, one hand on each side of the coffin. He knew that it would take a while to work the nails loose, and the extra weight of dirt might make this impossible. That was one of his biggest fears, to regain consciousness and be stuck, unable to move or act.

Exhaling, he pressed up against the lid, feeling the boards slowly move. By his head, he could hear a nail straining to work its way free. That was it? There were no other nails to be pried free around his head? Why was there only a single nail? Had someone figured out his secret?

His mind swam as he imagined a lynch mob waiting above for him. What he had thought of as lamplight could actually be flickering torches, the Sheriff waiting with four ropes this time. They would have him drawn and quartered to make sure he was dead.

His strength faltered at the thought and the lid came back down. Realizing that he hadn't heard any more dirt in the last minute, it all but confirmed his suspicion. They were waiting for him and here he was, defenseless, with less wind in him than a newborn baby. He felt the sudden need to escape; perhaps, if he moved quickly enough, he could gain the element of surprise. That wouldn't buy him much time though, and he knew it.

A sudden and intense sense of impotence filled him, the same way it had as he had lain suffering in that small shanty years before. The sense of loss as he had watched his parents pass from consumption. The uncertainty, the sadness, the paralyzing fear of how he'd survive.

He found himself wishing that he could curl up into the fetal position and cry, as he had that night so many years ago. Yet in that moment instinct kicked in, his fight or flight reflex switching itself over to fight.

More blood oozed before he realized what was happening his arms pushed, lifting the lid, his legs following in one fluid movement. He didn't have time to recognize what was at the top of the hole, his brain wasn't responding to any normal thought. Instead, his fingers were digging into the dirt sides of the grave, using anything they could grasp as a handhold to pull him to the surface.

"See, that's the problem with this kind of job. The blacksmith, the general store, even the farmers are all in as soon as it's dark. But we're expected to finish the job they hired us for even if it takes all night," said Tim, sitting on a pile of dirt that had been removed from the grave. Patch recognized his voice from when he'd come to dig a well at Sally's place last year.

"You know we could have come up here earlier, like this morning when the sheriff came in and asked us to dig this hole. Then we'd be having a few drinks by now," the other man's nasally voice made him sound like the younger of the two. In the light Patch couldn't tell though, they were merely two shadowy silhouettes in the pale moonlight.

"Drinks are the easy part, and that's why I called you over. This tequila won't drink itself."

Patch crested the edge of the grave as Tim passed the bottle to the nasally sounding man. His motions, entirely running on reflex, snatched the man closest to him by the neck before giving his head a twist. As the bottle fell to the ground, its contents dampening the dusty earth, Patch released the man. The body spun behind him like a top and fell into the open grave with a crash.

Tim stared at him, as if he were some fiery demon from the bowels of hell. Patch grabbed the front of his shirt and began to rip, buttons flying and bouncing as he did so.

"You-- you-- you were-- I saw you--" the man stammered. Patch could see Tim's eyes were on the verge of leaping from their sockets.

The cool of the night air plucked at the moisture on his chest as blood seeped from the opening ribs. The black tendrils inside him began their little trick, ejecting the shredded heart from its spot and preparing for a new one.

23

Patch watched as Tim stumbled backwards towards the shovel. Patch's strength was fading, the frenzied action from the climb out had taken more wind from him than he would have thought. Patch crushed the blackened mass of muscle that had once been his heart, as he lunged at Tim. Forming his hand so that his fingers were pressed together tightly and pointing straight out, he punched through the man's stomach. Blood spurting as his fingernails dug. The muscle of the abdomen resisted before his fingers found purchase on the quivering organ.

Like plucking an apple, he pulled and twisted, feeling a slight resistance as he removed his hand. The man had been screaming, he realized, as he secured the fresh heart among his own organs. The cries hadn't registered until he felt the first life-giving beat.

Glancing down at his chest, he watched as black tendrils tucked everything into place before pulling the cavity closed. As the two sides of the ribs met he took a deep breath, the wind returning almost instantly to his limbs. The adrenaline that was still present in the heart made him feel alive.

Staring down the path towards the few buildings below he waited. He knew that if the screams were heard, someone would be on their way up to check it out soon. He crouched and picked up the bottle of tequila to take a swig. It was hardly enough to wet his tongue, but he was grateful to get the musty taste out of his mouth.

After a few minutes passed, the plateau had fallen silent and he decided no one was coming. Without a second thought he climbed back into the hole to retrieve the other man's shirt.

* * * * *

The sun was rising as he sat next to the pick and shovels. Patch knew this was when he should move on, to head somewhere else where he was an unknown, but that didn't feel right.

As he had worked, something had trickled into his memory; the voice of the Sheriff and Samuel talking about something that involved Sally and her work. What bothered him is that he couldn't figure out where the fragments of conversation had come from. He couldn't think of when he'd ever seen James Roberts and Samuel together at any given time. The thought of leaving her high and dry didn't seem right.

Besides, he had a bone to pick with the sheriff. He would have probably fallen unconscious from the hanging soon enough. There was no reason for him to shoot; you don't shoot captive prisoners if you have any honor.

Standing, he began to walk out of town and away from the people who had watched him die. He had to figure this out, something needed to be done and he had to decide what that was.

Travis Coleman

CHAPTER 5

The smell of bacon frying nudged Sally to her senses. At first she felt disoriented, the last thought she could remember was looking out of the window at the moon. The thought of sleep had been distant, much like everything had felt yesterday.

The whole day had been spent cleaning, washing, and setting fleeces out to dry. Today it was another day of shearing the sheep which Samuel had brought down from the pasture. At least that didn't require much focus. Her job was more to supervise and help pick out what hay and burrs might be in the wool. It was perfect for the way she was feeling, something that came automatically to her and required little thought.

Her thoughts were still dwelling on the events of the other night. What had she been thinking? Walking up to the sheriff with a loaded weapon was going to cause problems. She had felt sick when she woke up yesterday and had hardly eaten, but the smell of bacon now perfuming the air left her stomach grumbling.

Slowly she got out of bed and began to dress, her mind flipping through her actions again. She remembered that she had sent Samuel into town for Patrick's personal effects, the bundle now lay open on the chair in the corner. As she picked up her brush from the vanity she could see his belt buckle sitting there and a part of her wanted to reach out and touch it.

"Stupid," she chided herself quietly. It wasn't like her to talk to herself. She was always so self-composed and in control. Yet in her mind the canvas of regret was being painted over and over again with portraits of "What if." What if she'd told him about how she felt? Would he have been interested in her? Would they have had a future together? What if she had offered to let him stay in the house that night instead of sending him back to the bunkhouse?

The thought made her shudder, not the thought of holding him close, but of what Emma might have gone through had Patrick not been on his way out. What would she have had to endure?

She'd known Deputy Smith since he'd been Little William Smith. Even back in the school yard he'd been nefarious for trying to peek up girls skirts. Often he'd even push them down to take a gander, the man had been little more than a pervert his entire life. What might he have done to Emma?

Shaking her head she tried to focus on what she was doing. Drawing the brush through her hair, clearing out the knots, that was what was important. Once she had her hair pulled back and tied with a ribbon, she opened her door.

The food only smelled better once the door opened, and she wondered where the bacon came from. There hadn't been any rashers of bacon left earlier this week. They were going to do without until time came to slaughter some of the pigs. As she made it to the foot of the stairs she was even more surprised to see the girls setting up a loom in the spinning room.

"What are you doing? We still have to spin the wool." She asked. The girls all paused looking at her. The one closest to her, Mary, finally spoke up explaining.

"Samuel said that since we still had yarn we should start another blanket." She stated. The other girls looked on, uncertain of whether they should continue setting things up.

"Girls, Samuel is in charge of the sheep, not the looms. While I understand he has a point, we need some of the dyed wool to make sure our colors match. There is a reason that, this month, I don't want you girls weaving. We have a garden to bring in, wool to clean, and soon we'll also have pork to cure." The girls didn't respond, instead they began to take apart pieces of the loom which they had already connected.

"So, where is Samuel? I'd like to chat with him." she asked the question before realizing that there were still cooking noises coming from the kitchen. As Mary began to motion towards the kitchen she heard his voice from behind her.

"I thought you were going to sleep all day. I hoped that the bacon would help wake you." Samuel sounded excited to be there.

"Is there a problem in the stable hand's kitchen?" she asked, turning to face him. She could feel her mouth tightening into a frown. This was not what she wanted to deal with this morning. Her home had rules, and schedules. To her it was place of order. When storms raged outside, when there were reports of bandits or some wild animal in the area, this was her place of refuge. This was the place that made sense to her.

"No, there's no problem. I know you've been having a hard time dealing with the loss of Patrick and so I decided I'd step in to help out. You know, cook some breakfast, keep the girls busy." He poured a cup of coffee from the pot and offered it to her.

"They don't need to be kept busy," she snapped at him. Instantly she regretted it, he looked like he had been slapped. Behind her she could hear the faint scuffling of feet as the girls tried to make themselves scarce. The whole atmosphere of the room was suddenly tense and nervous. "I mean..."

Pausing she took a deep breath and tried to collect her thoughts. What was it that bothered her so much about his presence? Was it his presence that was bothering her?

"Samuel, you're great, but right now there is just so much chaos flying around. We lost a good farm hand, one of my girls was attacked, plus it is the busy time of the year as we prepare for the winter. While I appreciate your help, I need things to stay in the order that we've established."

When she spoke the words, tears to welled up in her eyes. She watched as he turned and walked to the kitchen. With a sigh she followed him only to find him walking with a plate full of food towards the door.

"What are you doing?" she asked as he reached for the door handle.

"I guess my food isn't good enough for you?" He practically spit as he said it. "I figured I'd take it out to the hogs, let them eat it so you can go back to what's normal."

"I didn't say that!" her outburst caused him to freeze with his hand on the door knob.

"Well then what did you mean? I think it's clear that I'm just trying to be there for you, to help you out, and you're throwing it back in my face. Yes I know it's creating a bit of disorder, but I'm handling it."

He slammed the plate onto the table, scrambled eggs falling over the edge onto the table cloth. Sally had to fight her initial reaction to scoop the eggs back onto the plate. Instead she focused on him, she'd never seen Samuel so emotional about anything.

"Samuel, I don't know if it needs to be handled. We need..." she began but Samuel continued talking.

"Jacob is already getting the sheep ready to shear. He wants to pick up some slack and stay on through the winter. He likes it here and wants to work with the herds next summer as well. We'll wash the fleeces at night to free up your girls from the work..."

Her sigh broke his train of thought. As she did it she collapsed into a chair and stared at the table cloth.

"What?" he demanded, his tone making his mood clear.

"You don't understand what I'm trying to do here do you?" she began. Looking up at him she could see the anger in his eyes had faded to confusion.

"There is a reason that I have this setup the way I do. Many of these girls will go on to get married, have children, and some may end up widowed. These girls didn't have parents to raise them and teach them all the little things you need to know to live life. That is why they wash the wool, that is why they spin it, that is why they weave. The last place I want them to end up is in a brothel."

Samuel turned his back on her, his arms resting on his hips as he stared out the kitchen window. She knew he was listening, it was one of the things she knew he did well. There were just times that she needed someone to listen.

"But if they don't find a suitor, should they end up alone, I want them to have this knowledge. I want them to be able to be strong and take care of themselves. That's why they have the chores. That is why we don't go buy bacon from the butcher. That is why we don't weave right now."

He began to pace at this and she watched him. A part of her wanted to pull the plate of food over and begin eating it. The bacon did smell delicious but she knew it would undermine what she had said. So instead she waited for some kind of a reaction.

Samuel reached for the door handle again, without turning he muttered to her. "I'll go let Jacob know."

With that he stepped out the door, slamming it behind him. The glass in the window shuddered and for a moment Sally was certain it would break.

As she watched him walk away her fingers found their way to the food. She felt bad that she was eating this after what she'd told him, but to waste food that had already been prepared would be wrong.

There was one thing that was good about the argument she realized as she ate a fork full of the eggs. Her mind had been diverted. But where had this change come from in Samuel's behavior?

This wasn't anything like the Samuel she'd known for years. Had the attack really upset him this much? Was he just trying to protect her?

Echoes of a hammer against the anvil told her that Samuel wasn't happy with the way things had gone. The way that he was reacting made her feel uneasy. She hoped it was nerves and would go away soon. But she knew that she would be leaving the shotgun next to her bed tonight.

Travis Coleman

CHAPTER 6

Thomas climbed the road to the plateau, as the sun slowly set over his shoulder . He'd been looking for Jonah all afternoon but no one had seen him, not since he had left to dig the grave yesterday.

Jonah was supposed to take the wagon into Santa Fe with Thomas to pick up lumber tomorrow. It was going to take two days for the trip, yet they couldn't leave if he couldn't be found today.

Thomas had been looking forward to this trip for a while now to go visit his family. There had also been talk of visiting a brothel for their overnight stay. It wasn't that he actively wanted to seek out the place, but the way the Sheriff and Peter talked about it, he needed that experience to give him confidence.

Perhaps once he had been with a woman they'd start taking him seriously. Was that too much to ask for? Then could they listen to his ideas without telling him he was an idiot?

Shaking his head he brought his focus back to what he was doing. He needed to find Jonah; that was all. Nothing else mattered. But what if Jonah had disappeared?

Something about that thought unsettled him. Until a week ago the community had been stagnant. Rarely did people move into, or out of, their small town. He'd been the last person to arrive about a year ago. About a year before it had been Patrick. Now Patrick was dead, the deputy was dead, and Jonah and Timothy were missing.

As he crested the top of the plateau he saw the graveyard spread out east of the road, with the ragged lines of tombstones standing in defiance to the desert sky. A sign hung from the arch, the word "Cemetery" in dirty white letters, with crosses ornamenting either side. Off in the distance, about a mile further up the road, he could see the bell tower of the mission.

His eyes traced the route from that bell tower back towards the cemetery and settled on a horse with two riders passing beneath the arch. He cupped his hands over his eyes to try to make out who was riding the horse, but at this distance he could only recognize the horse they were riding. He'd seen it two nights ago at the lynching. It was Miss Sally's horse.

He arched his brows and continued walking towards the cemetery, though he was uncertain of who was riding the horse, he knew Miss Sally always wore a straw hat when she came into town. It was something that could be counted on, like the heat in July. They also appeared to be wearing dresses from this distance, which told him it wasn't Samuel or Jacob.

Were these the girls that Miss Sally was raising? Sheriff Roberts had always made them sound like a bunch of small girls, none of them old enough to let go of their mother's apron strings. These girls were well into their teens, not what he'd pictured at all.

The sun was nearing the horizon to his left; shielding his eyes he continued his approach. The presence of the girls made him wonder why they were here? Lines of events began to form in his head like strands of spider silk floating on the wind. The presence of Samuel in the shop yesterday began to take on a more sinister edge.

Had they sent him there to find out when the body would be moved? Perhaps they had laid in wait, riding in from the mission to ambush Tim and Jonah. Had they stolen the body to take back and bury on their own?

The story began to deviate as he approached the arch. Now the body was being revived by some ancient magic. Perhaps these two were lying in wait for him now, kidnapping anyone who came close to the graveyard.

He didn't want to admit it, but he was suddenly scared of these two girls and their actions. He took a good look at the girls now that he was closer; one of them was barely into her teenage years. While he was only nineteen, he knew that that age wouldn't matter if they had a gun. The shots from Sally's shotgun rang out inside his head all over again. He stumbled slightly at the thought, kicking rocks and dirt while he tried to catch his balance.

"You're not here to cause problems are you?" the older of the girls asked. She looked at him, keeping the reins of the horse close at hand. The other girl already had one foot in the stirrup, ready to climb up.

"No, I'm here looking for a friend of mine. He was supposed to bury Patrick. But we haven't seen him since we dropped off the coffin." Thomas added. He watched as the older girl placed her hand on the younger girl's shoulder.

"It's okay Emma," she said. Emma took her foot from the stirrup but still didn't let go of the saddle horn.

Thomas realized who the younger girl was. This was the girl the deputy had attacked. He felt two sets of emotions, unable to decide which of them fit the situation.

The deputy had been his friend, someone he had played cards with frequently. Had she not been around he might still be alive, but the feeling of anger and animosity towards this girl in her white skirt made him feel like some kind of monster.

The deputy had been a man of many faults, the best known was that he was a sore loser. There had been nights where half the people at the table had sworn off playing with him after he threw the deck. Despite that, he had still been a friend. To not feel something for the person who had been crucial to your friend's demise...

"So, are you going to quit staring at us so we can go about our business?" the older girl asked. He realized that he had been staring off in their direction.

"I'm so sorry, I didn't realize who you ladies were until now. As a friend of the Deputy, I want to apologize..." he stopped as the older girl pushed Emma behind the horse. She produced a small fruit knife from the apron she wore at her waist.

"You get out of here, we want nothing to do with you lot." she stated, brandishing the blade. Thomas stumbled backwards with the sudden movement.

"I didn't mean it like that. I just..." his mind went blank, his mouth continuing to stammer until he spit out the words. "I feel bad about what happened."

Silence hung in the air, neither party wanting to say anything. The older girl still stood in front of him, knife leveled directly at his chest. He was certain a minute passed before he heard the quiet voice of Emma coming from behind her.

"Mary, I don't think he meant it like that," Emma said. "He doesn't seem like the Deputy, he doesn't have that crazy look in his eyes."

Thomas nodded frantically, "I'm not like him, I only played cards with him."

The knife began to bob before falling to her side. Thomas didn't bother to put his hand down, he didn't move at all.

"Can you go sit over there so we can pay our respects? We only want to say goodbye to Patrick. Then we'll be on our way and you can do whatever it is you came to do," Mary stated as she dropped the fruit knife back into the safety of her apron.

Emma had already stepped over to the grave and knelt down beside it. He could hear her crying, and in that moment his theory of Jonah's kidnapping fell apart. These girls weren't involved in some plot. They were experiencing the loss as much as anyone else in the community.

Pangs of guilt assaulted his senses, he could feel tears welling up in the corners of his eyes. "I'm sorry if I said the wrong thing Mary. I feel like the whole town has been turned upside down in a matter of days. I shouldn't... "

He paused, uncertain of exactly what he wanted to say. Should he bring up the deputy? Would that end up with another knife drawn on him?

"I'm just sorry for your loss. I wish I hadn't interrupted your grieving."

Mary nodded her head and then waited patiently as Emma knelt next to the grave. It became obvious to Thomas that this was for Emma, coming to pay her respects to the man who saved her that night.

Something about that resonated in him in a way all the card playing and drinking he normally experienced didn't. There was something honest and open about the way these girls treated him. They hadn't kept secrets from him the way others did at the shop. In his heart he felt he could trust them.

Thomas and Mary stood there until the bell at the mission tolled dusk. As the bell rang Mary spoke, "Emma, we need to go. It's late and the horse may hurt itself in the dark if we don't hurry."

"I'll be right there," her voice quivered as she did her best to hide what was left of her tears. Thomas realized he hadn't seen anything up here that might indicate where his friend had gone.

"If you'd like I'll walk you home," Thomas said quietly turning to face Mary. He didn't know why he had offered. He was supposed to be back at the shop to prepare for the trip to Santa Fe tomorrow, not roaming around the countryside.

"I know you don't have a reason to trust me, but I don't want anyone else to get hurt. Especially if I could prevent it," he stated. He didn't look directly at them, choosing instead to look at their feet as they stepped up to the horse.

Emma placed her foot in the stirrup and swung back into the saddle. Meanwhile, Mary gathered the reins and tossed them to Thomas.

"We both would appreciate it. The last few days have been trying on all of us," Mary said before pulling herself up into the saddle. Emma sat in front and clung tightly to the saddle horn.

"I'll make sure you get home safe." Thomas promised and led the horse out through the arch. He turned right, towards the mission, and made his way towards Sally's farm.

Travis Coleman

CHAPTER 7

The sheriff hung limply from the tree, slowly spinning in the cool night air. His eyes flicked open, though it took a few moments before he showed any sign that he understood where he was.

"Hello, Sheriff," Patch exclaimed. He watched as Sheriff Roberts' face went through various emotions. Confusion was first as though he had never heard the voice before, then anger as he began to realize the situation he was in, before it faded back to confusion as his eyes focused on Patch.

Patch had hung him from a tree far outside of town. His arms bound tightly against his sides leaving him immobile. The Sheriff struggled against the restraints trying to get them to come free, but they held secure. Then a look of realization crossed his face. Patch watched as he tried to spit one of the gravedigger's socks out of his mouth.

"Hold on, I need to make a few things clear. First off, if I pull that sock out of your mouth and you scream, I'll slit your throat. If you lie to me, I'll kill you too."

The Sheriff renewed his struggle, trying to find a way to get free. His revolution became erratic and Patch stepped back to watch.

"Now, I'm going to show you I mean business before I remove the gag from your mouth." With this Patch stepped up to the Sheriff and pulled the knife from his boot.

The Sheriff's eyes widened as he saw the moonlight gleam off of the blade. Before he could react further, Patch grabbed him and spun him to face the trunk.

"This will only take a minute, but you'll get the message either way." Patch whispered into his ear as he began carving into the man's exposed shoulders.

Letters began to form, first a C followed by an O. The muffled screams began to get louder, as though the sock might be coming loose. Patch spun him around again and used the knife blade to force the cloth back into his mouth.

"I'm sorry to say, but if you spit that out I'll make sure you can't scream anymore by cutting out your tongue." He grinned, and he could tell that it disturbed the Sheriff. The slow trickle of urine that now speckled the dirt confirmed it.

With a spin Patch twisted him around and started the letter W. The flesh parted, blood welled up into the cuts. The rope was already beginning to show a slight tinge of crimson from the first two letters.

Sheriff Roberts still squirmed and writhed in pain, but he no longer seemed to be trying to spit out the sock. Patch had almost finished the D before he heard the quiet sobs coming from the man. Finishing the cuts, he then spun the Sheriff to face him again.

"Now, no matter what happens here tonight, everyone will know you for the coward that you are. Any woman that you decide to sleep with will know the character of the man she took into her bed."

The words had no effect on the Sheriff this time. The fight had left him. The tears created shining lines down his cheeks and his shoulders were slumped in defeat.

"Now, I need to know something. I have a memory in my head of you talking to Samuel, something about Miss Sally's ranch."

The Sheriff's head snapped up, the tears still rimming his eyes. That hadn't been a reaction Patch had expected.

"So, you know something about that?" Patch asked as he reached for the gag. He held the knife at the throat so he could cut the vocal cords if needed. As he pulled the sock loose he choked a bit at the smell.

"You're dead, this has to be some kind of nightmare," Sheriff Roberts began. "I shot you through the heart, you had bled out."

"Sorta," Patch interrupted. "This isn't a dream, you did shoot me, and I still have the scar to prove it."

He lifted his shirt up so the Sheriff could see the scar on his back, just below the rib cage. It still oozed slightly despite being filled with black clots.

"How?" was all the Sheriff could utter before his mouth ceased to work. Patch turned back to him, letting his shirt fall.

"To be honest, I don't know. The important thing is, I'm about to remove the last of the law in this town if you don't start answering some questions. Now, as I said, what were you and Samuel talking about?" he asked.

Patch watched as Sheriff Roberts mouthed words, unable to form any sound. Patch tried to make it out by reading his lips, but the lantern was too dim.

"Come on," Patch shouted before punching him in the gut. There was a sharp intake of breath, but still nothing came from the Sheriff's mouth. "Have it your way then."

Patch took the knife in one hand and grasped the man's little finger. He made a single cut from the tip to the knuckle and began to peel back the skin.

The screams began to echo, but Patch wasn't in a patient mood. This man had hung him, shot him, and tried to bury him, he deserved no mercy. Patch was prying the nail loose when the Sheriff's screams stopped and he began to talk.

"It was all Samuel's idea, okay? I wanted nothing to do with it! He wanted the ranch and promised to give us a blanket a year for sale. That's far more than we ever got from that whore Sally," he was stopped short as Patch stabbed him through the palm of his hand.

"Don't talk badly about women. Your mother was one and she'd be ashamed to hear you talk like that," Patch stated.

"You don't understand about Sally, she is a whore." The Sheriff looked Patch dead in the eyes as he said it. There was no sign of deceit that Patch could see.

"Look, don't use the word whore and I'll let you explain yourself. But if you say it again, I'll flay each of your fingers first," Patch grinned.

The Sheriff took a few labored breaths before beginning. "You don't know much about Sally's history do you? Why she ended up here or how she got the money for the ranch? When she was a girl she was orphaned. Her mother was Navajo and her dad was a Spanish trader."

"I knew what her heritage was, and I knew she was an orphan," Patch spat back at him and then stabbed his knife into the top of the sawhorse the lantern rested on.

"Well, when she was young her father was killed in an argument. There were years before she was abandoned to the church. Those were the years where her mother couldn't do enough to make ends meet. That's when she started sleeping with anyone who could pay," the Sheriff began to look around.

"Do you have anything to drink?" Sheriff Roberts asked. "My mouth tastes awful after that sock, and talking is making me thirsty."

Patch looked around for the bottle he had earlier, the one he'd taken from the grave digger. He'd refilled it with water, and it was better than nothing.

"Keep talking while I find the bottle, I know I left it around here somewhere," Patch stood and stretched. He waited for the man to continue before he began looking in earnest.

"Like I was saying her mom got to the point where no one would come around anymore. She'd be drunk most of the time, and that's when the sickness set in," he paused and smacked his lips.

"I'm looking" Patch muttered. Then he spotted the bottle nestled in the crook of a tree branch. He'd left it there while he'd dragged the Sheriff's unconscious body into the tree. Thankfully he'd been completely drunk when Patch had arrived at his home.

"Well, Sally's mom was pretty far gone when Sally finally was told to go to the mission. Her mother died alone in their hogan. The only thing she took with her was what her mother had taught her, her name, and the clothes on her back," the Sheriff paused as he saw Patch pull the bottle from the tree.

"I'd throw it to ya, but you're in no state to catch it," Patch remarked. He noted that the blood from the Sheriff's hand wasn't dripping. It congealed around the finger, but it didn't seem incredibly thick.

He tipped the bottle up to the Sheriff's lips and watched as he gulped it down. He drained about a quarter of the bottle before Patch pulled it away.

"More story, more water. But get to the future, I don't need to know all this history," Patch stated. He then plopped back down onto the stool he was seated on.

"Okay, the important bit is this. When she left the mission, instead of taking the vows and joining a convent, she didn't have anywhere to go. She only had two things that she knew, weaving and..." he let it hang in the air.

Patch didn't know what to think about this revelation. He'd always seen her as untouched like the Virgin Mary. Now he was seeing her as a woman who had lied to him. His life was a long list of gray areas with another lie compounding on top of it.

"I don't want to believe you, but you don't act like a liar. Most people won't try to spin a tale when their hide is on the line," Patch muttered. He picked up the bottle and took a swig, only to be disappointed that it was only water.

"Well, here is the most interesting bit, she only did it for about a year before she got her little home setup. Samuel brought her money but never... sampled the wares. I did, and I can say that she was good. I even asked her if she'd consider being my wife, but she shot that idea down."

The Sheriff began to laugh this time, though he quickly found himself coughing. His body wanted to fold itself over, but the rope didn't allow anything of the sort.

"She said she couldn't marry someone who paid for her... " Another fit of coughing broke the sentence.

Patch noticed that despite the water, the blood hadn't begun to drip again. For all he knew the water he'd given him had flowed into the lungs.

"Finish what you were saying," Patch said. His voice came out almost shouting and he was surprised at how tense he sounded.

"You see, Samuel felt he was owed something for getting her out of that life. But Miss Sally, she saw it as another man trying to pay her and wanted nothing to do with him," the Sheriff's voice almost gave out as he talked.

"So, you're saying he feels like something is owed to him and has come to collect?" Patch blurted out.

The Sheriff did his best to nod on the rope. Patch stood up and began to walk away from the tree. As the lantern light began to move away the Sheriff began to speak.

"Cut... cut me down..."

Patch paused and looked over his shoulder. "You've lost too much blood, you're going to bleed out. Hope you've got something inside you like I've got in me. Then perhaps we'll meet again."

Patch continued to walk, the Sheriff trying his best to call out to him. It didn't matter, now he understood what he'd overheard. The worst part about it was that someone he had trusted had put it in motion.

In his mind he could see the face of Emma as the the Deputy had loomed over her. That look played across the faces of the rest of the girls and it infuriated him. Yesterday he'd been dead, but today he was alive with a vengeance.

CHAPTER 8

The cool of the night was burning away as Thomas rolled out of bed. By the time he'd escorted Mary and Emma out to the ranch, it had been too dark to head back into town. They'd been nice enough to let him crash in the bunkhouse, but it'd taken him forever to fall asleep. He'd faced the wall for the first little bit but he was certain that the other two men were watching him.

Why had he bothered to walk the girls out here? The road had been even, there had been no danger at all, but he'd done it anyway.

Mary, the slight smile she'd given him in an apology came unbidden to his mind. The corners of his mouth twitched as he pulled his boots on, but he shook his head to clear his mind. He needed to get back to town before Peter started throwing a fit and burning the few possessions that he had.

The thought of his possessions in the fire didn't matter much. Then he remembered the small box that his father had given him. Inside were the tools that his grandfather had passed on to him. While his father hadn't become a full carpenter, deciding instead to carve out a piece of the land, his grandfather had been amazing. Those tools had crossed the plains with his father and had been what was used to fashion the house he'd been raised in. The thought of his grandfather's tools lying among the embers, becoming brittle and useless, lit a fire under him.

He pulled on his other boot and then reached for his hat when he heard a rapping on the wooden frame of the door. He turned to the doorway but could only see a squat shadow in the light.

"I'd really like to know why you came out here last night," he heard Sally ask. As she stepped around the door frame and into the room he saw she was holding her trusty shotgun in one hand.

"Miss Sally, I only wanted to make sure they got home safe," Thomas stated. He backed up slowly, not realizing that he was raising his hands out to his sides.

"You know, I don't like you or your friends. After what happened with the Deputy I'd almost rather not have any men around here," Sally didn't level the gun, but she did bring it across so that it rested easily between her two hands. Thomas knew that it would take only a moment for her to shoulder the gun. He took a deep breath and slowly exhaled, hoping that the motion wouldn't cause her to draw.

"I told Mary last night, they're only friends because that's who I work with. Kind of like you're friends with Samuel and those girls you have. I don't always see eye to eye with the things they do. The Deputy's actions are a perfect example," Thomas was a bit surprised that he'd spoken the words so well, in his head they'd been a jumbled mess. When he'd opened his mouth he'd felt certain she'd shoot him for stammering.

"That sounds like a good story, but you aren't welcome here," Sally's face was finally visible now that his eyes had adjusted to the light. Her face seemed to belong to some ancient statue which had weathered and cracked.

"I'm sorry that I did a good deed and wanted to make sure these girls got back here okay. I'm leaving this morning and heading back to town," Thomas replied and pointed towards the door. "I won't come back without an invitation if you let me leave in peace."

She watched him as he started to make his way towards the door. Then with a sigh she turned and walked out of the room ahead of him. He paused, not wanting to make any sudden moves as she left.

He felt relieved once she was gone, the gun had brought a lot of unnecessary stress into the situation. At that moment he realized that he'd only been moments away from losing bladder control.

"If she'd shouldered the shotgun," he muttered under his breath. That would have done it, would have left him standing in a puddle of his own creation, but at least it was over now.

He stepped out into the light, shielding his eyes as they adjusted. He could see Miss Sally making her way towards the door of the house; Samuel was on her heels talking as they walked. Her face hadn't changed though. It was still stern and resolute.

Thomas turned and walked to the outhouse, the only place that he had planned to stop before he made his way back to town. His visit was quick and then he began his trip.

He knew that Peter would be angry that he'd been out all night. He knew that he'd be late for the trip to Santa Fe. For all he knew he had a shotgun trained on him as he walked away. The deck seemed to be stacked against him no matter how he tried to look at the hand he was dealt. If it'd been a real card game he'd have folded.

He peered back over his shoulder to make sure there wasn't a pointing gun at him, and then settled into a steady gait. His stomach growled and his mouth tasted like the dust of the road. A part of him wanted to turn back and get a drink from the well. But he knew that if he kept going he could drink at the mission.

He scanned the sky to the west hoping to see some kind of clouds along the horizon, but was disappointed. It seemed he would get no relief, so he continued in silence.

His thoughts drifted back to his walk the night before. Though the trip had been dark it hadn't seemed oppressive. The company had made the journey feel short and they'd laughed several times, including when he'd tripped on a stone he hadn't seen. He knew that part of what had made him feel so good had been Mary. Looking back to see her smile draped in her dark brown curls.

Their introduction had gone about as far from good as one could go without blood being drawn; yet the strength she'd shown had made her more attractive. He knew where he stood with her and that made him feel like it was the best relationship he'd formed since he left home.

Everyone he was surrounded with seemed to be keeping things from him. Sheriff Roberts, Peter, Samuel, they all seemed to have some self-serving motives that they wouldn't tell him about. He didn't realize it was a problem at first, he had only come to learn a trade, but living a life without trust and honesty had left him looking for something.

The thunder of hoof beats from behind him brought him out of his thoughts. He spun around and faced the rider who was approaching quickly from behind. Dust spun around her and once she got closer he could see a small bundle cradled in her lap.

"Mary," he exclaimed. She was the last person that he expected to see. He'd half expected it to be Samuel, coming to put the screws to him about what he'd told Sally. He didn't know much but knew that Samuel had been plotting with the Sheriff. That probably would be enough to fetch a beating from the man.

"You didn't come in for breakfast," she said as she reigned in the horse. The animal was sweating and had been ridden hard from the ranch behind him. He stepped towards her and patted the horse on the shoulder softly before responding.

"I didn't feel welcome there, so I didn't want to make a nuisance of myself," Thomas knew it sounded stupid. Telling her that Sally had shown up at his bed with a shotgun wouldn't be much better.

"We saw her head out there, but we didn't realize she told you to leave. Emma and I woke up early and made extra biscuits. The least we could do is feed you for walking us back." She raised the small bundle and motioned that she was going to throw it.

Thomas waited for, and then caught the offered bundle. He could smell the biscuits and saw a slight sheen on the top. Had they been topped with butter? His mouth was already salivating and he snapped his first bite. He was two bites in before he realized that he had nothing to rinse them down with. He heard Mary giggling as she watched him eat.

"I need something to drink," he tried to say though it came out sounding like he was choking, the words almost impossible to say around the doughy mess. She began to titter again as he tried to say more. He gave up trying to speak and instead mimed tilting his head back as though drinking. She realized what he was saying and offered a hand up.

"Come on, I'll give you a ride as far as the mission. We can get you some water there," she stated as he took her hand. He noticed how soft her skin was right away, as his own calloused and scarred hand slid like sandpaper against her palm. Once he was astride the horse he faced a new dilemma, where to put his hands.

"Where can I...?" he began to ask, this time spitting crumbs as he spoke. She didn't hesitate though and took his arms, guiding him to hold her around the waist.

"It's okay, I know you don't mean anything by it. Besides, I am used to riding with a second person with me," as his arms tightened around her she brought the horse up to a trot. The pace seemed a bit fast and Thomas found himself wondering if the horse could handle it with two riders. She was oblivious to his worry and soon her hair was bouncing on her shoulders and into his face.

He finally managed to swallow and took the opportunity to call out to her, "Do you think this is too fast for the horse?"

"No, we're supposed to exercise him each day to make sure she stays healthy. Besides, I want to be on my way back as soon as possible. Sally would be cross with me if she knew I was out here with you," she paused and Thomas found himself wanting an explanation. Would she be disowned and cast out of the ranch if she was caught?

He began to worry about the consequences as he'd only just met this girl. If she were banned from going to her home where would she go? Would she end up staffing the railing at some brothel? Would he be willing to take care of her with the little he had? What did he have?

He began to go through a mental list of the few possessions he had, sure that it wouldn't be enough to provide for the two of them. But what was he thinking? He'd met this girl yesterday, they weren't courting, they were barely even acquaintances.

"What is that?" Mary asked back over her shoulder. She motioned ahead to a tree a little ways off the road. Something dangled from the branches and a few items were scattered around it.

"I don't know, but I'm pretty sure it wasn't there last night." he replied. Whatever was at the end of the rope was spinning slightly as they approached. As they got closer his mouth dried out as though he'd crammed all of the biscuits into his mouth at once.

"Is that...?" Mary's voice quivered in horror and he understood why. They'd both seen the word coward carved into the back of the person hanging, and as the man had rotated they'd finally recognized who it was.

"Yeah, that's Sheriff Roberts," Thomas croaked.

Travis Coleman

CHAPTER 9

Sally stepped into the light and let the shotgun's muzzle fall back to the ground. Without thinking she pumped the lever and verified that she didn't have a shell in the gun. Thankfully she hadn't needed it. Thomas didn't act like the rest of the sheriff's crew.

She saw a dust devil pushing a piece of brush across the yard. A part of her felt like something else should be happening, like a storm should have started in that room. But the relative calm of the desert around her told a different story. It felt like the calm before the storm. Any moment a tornado, or lightning storm, or something nasty would blow through. Instead she walked back over to the house. There was wool to work with inside and she needed to keep busy.

"Sally!" Samuel called to her. She rolled her eyes as she turned to greet him.

"What do you need Samuel?" she asked him, pausing to let him approach. She didn't want to deal with more of his crap, having the boy here had been bad enough. When you added the way he had acted yesterday before storming out of the house she almost wished the gun were loaded.

"Sally, so what are we doing with the boy? Do I need to build a gallows?" he grinned as he said it.

The grin sent shivers down her spine. A few days ago that smile had been reassuring. He had been calm, cool, collected, and most of all pleasant to be around. The yelling had brought back too many unwanted memories.

She was a little girl again on the dirt floor of the hogan. Her mother tried to defend herself from the blows her father rained down on her. Her mother's lips bled, her left eye had swollen shut, and the only thing that remained constant were the shouts of her father. She had stared at her parents, not understanding all the words he was saying as she saw the dark fleck behind her mother move. It had been an old spear of her mothers that he'd broken over his knee.

Sally's father-she couldn't even remember his name anymore-stepped away from her for only a moment. It was only an instant, yet with one quick movement it was done. The flint spearhead and the six inches of the shaft sailed through the air. He was turning as the spear plunged deep into his side. Then came the blood, and the night became a blur. She still saw it in her dreams on stormy winter nights.

"Go away Samuel. The boy is leaving," she snapped and turned back towards the door. He didn't follow right away. Instead, he seemed dumbstruck by her response. Almost a full meter had opened up before he strode after her.

"What do you mean you're letting him go? He's like the deputy isn't he? Coming out here to take advantage of all the girls we..."

Sally spun and stared at him, his words freezing in his throat. She clenched the gun tighter and hoped that he didn't force her to use it.

"Look, I don't know what's transpired already. I don't know why the deputy decided to come out here and try to take advantage of my girls. Maybe the Sheriff told him of my old life. Maybe he was drunk and couldn't control himself." She paused, unsure of what she was going to say next.

"I know why he did it. He saw you as weak without a man around here to run the place. I'm sure your time in the brothel didn't exactly..." This time it was the gun that shut him up. She pulled the lever and reached for her apron pocket where she kept the shells.

"You don't know when to stop running your mouth Samuel. It'll be the death of you! Now you get back to your duties or I'll..." Sally's face was red and her words caught in her throat. She was flustered when she realized there weren't any shells in her pocket.

She spun rather than to let him gloat at her anger. This was an anger she hadn't felt in years, similar to the black rage that her father had so often fallen into.

As she climbed the stairs she heard him behind her approaching. His heavy footfalls sounding clearly on the hard packed dirt.

"You'll what!" he said as he reached for her arm. She didn't stop though, instead barging through the door and into the entry hall. She knew that the shells were there in a pouch just inside the door. Perhaps the storm she had been expecting had begun.

The door slammed behind the two of them and she felt him grip the gun trying to wrestle it from her grip.

"You're not going to shoot me Sally, we've been through too much together. I'm tired of you ignoring me and walking away. Today you're going to listen," he snarled at her. The distance between the two of them was now only the shotgun; both her hands clung to it with a white knuckled grip. But they both knew he was stronger than her, it was only a matter of time.

"Samuel, let go of me!" she cried back, trying to retain her grip with all her might. "You're a better man than this."

"Am I?" he spat back at her. "I've been there for you. I've fought for you and your livelihood. I have given you my earnings to help you realize this dream and you've snubbed me. Don't you understand that I love you Sally? I've loved you since we were at the mission together."

She tried to back into the kitchen, and he turned to follow him. She knew the cast iron skillet should be on the stove, if she could only reach it.

"You didn't want to love me back, saw me as another Jon coming to give my two dollars and take my time with you. I'm better than that, and I didn't judge you for your actions."

Her left hand fell free of the gun, unable to hold on any longer. Now her eyes looked over her shoulder, hoping that perhaps Mary would be there to place the skillet in her hands.

"Mary! Mary please!" she cried, but there was no response from the kitchen. She and Emma had made breakfast and should have been doing clean up now. Mary was supposed to be there.

"Shut up!" Samuel yelled and pulled the gun free from her hands. Sally spun backwards before falling onto the kitchen floor. To her surprise the kitchen was empty, the skillet lay on the table.

She began to crawl towards where they kept the knife, hoping that perhaps with that she could defend herself.

"I'm done waiting around for you Sally, so instead I'm going to run this place and you're going to listen for a while. I said I loved you, but you seem incapable of love."

The last statement made her stop moving and feel cold. She'd never been struck by words that rang more true. She'd been called names, been attacked by men and women, but this struck right in the heart.

The only sound in the room was their heavy breathing, both of them trying to regain their lost breath. This gave her a moment to think, was she really capable of love? Had she ever really loved anyone? Even Patrick she'd been uncertain about, but he had been the closest to love that she'd ever felt.

Her chest ached, the pain of the all the loss she'd felt in her life crushing down on her. The faces of her mother, her father, the child she'd borne during her time in the brothel, and Patrick all came to her. They were all dead now, each of them tore at her until she couldn't move anymore. She wanted to cry, wanted to release the hurt she was feeling, but her eyes were as dry as the desert outside.

"I'm sorry," she muttered as loudly as she could.

"You're sorry? Sorry for what? Not loving me despite everything I've done for you? You and I both know that if I had wanted you I could have had you back then. But I didn't want you bought and I don't want your pity now that I've finally spelled it out for you."

She could hear Samuel's footsteps stepping away from her but she didn't move for fear of angering him. There was no rustle from the cloth pouch inside the door, he wasn't after shells, he was only pacing.

While she listened, her mind turned over what he had said. Was it only pity she was feeling? Was she trying to buy herself time so she could escape? The chair she kept by the door slid over next to her. The butt of the gun rested on the ground as Samuel sat down beside her.

"You know I don't need you any more, keeping you around will only help keep the girls in line. If I decide to I could force the girls to work all day producing more of those blankets. The sheriff would turn a blind eye as long as he got what he wanted. Mostly some of the money and his choice of the girls from time to time."

She watched as Samuel leaned back, using the gun being as a prop to maintain his balance. Slowly she rolled onto her side, exposing her stomach to the man.

"But I'm willing to make a deal like we did before. This time I'll be calling the shots though. You handle the wool and weaving, I handle the..." his words fell into a shout as she lifted the front legs of the chair. She tried to pull herself onto her knees to continue the momentum; instead the butt of the gun caught her in the gut, knocking the wind out of her.

Sally fell to the floor again, this time sputtering and gasping for air. Samuel had fallen over backwards and was struggling to untangle himself from the chair. As she choked down the little air she could she realized this might be the last chance she would have to escape him. For all she knew this final act of defiance would be her last act alive.

The room began to spin, slowly at first, before darkening around the edges of her vision. Her arms wouldn't move the way she wanted them to, her legs were little more than noodles. The more she fought the more the darkness intruded on her vision. As it fully encompassed her, the last thin thread of hope which remained inside her, broke.

Travis Coleman

CHAPTER 10

Mary pressed the door handle, but couldn't get it to open. Behind her, Thomas strained to get Sheriff Roberts up the three steps to the door.

"It's not opening Thomas. Is it locked?" she asked. The truth was he didn't know if the door could lock. It was a problem that he had never had to deal with. Until yesterday he had spent almost all his time within yelling distance of Peter. Still he didn't remember any way to lock the door from the inside.

"Press down harder Mary. Hurry, I'm afraid I'll drop him and he's not breathing much." he gasped. The Sheriff's boots clicked against the bottom step as Thomas had the bulk of his weight resting on the small porch.

Mary continued trying in front of him, but he didn't know how much longer his arms would hold out. Getting him onto the horse and holding him there had been tough. He was surprised that the horse hadn't collapsed under the extra weight.

"It's still not..." Mary started before a click from the door silenced her.

"What do you want?" Peter started as he pulled open the door. "We want nothing to do..."

"Peter! Shut up and help me," Thomas snapped and pulled the Sheriff towards the door. Mary danced around Peter and made her way into the house.

Peter took one of the arms and watched as Thomas stepped to the other. That was when Peter saw the word carved into the Sheriff's back. "Oh dear lord, what happened to him?"

"Don't drop his arm!" Thomas yelled at him. Peter hesitated and then tightened his grip.

The two of them strained to move him through the door. As Thomas' eyes adjusted to the gloom inside he saw that Mary was at work in the kitchen. She'd cleared the table and was stoking the cooking fire in the stove.

"Let's get him on the table and take a look at him," Thomas instructed. Peter followed, though his eyes were still bulging from their sockets with shock. The movement inside the house was easy enough, and it wasn't until Peter tried to lift him onto the table face first that Thomas had to take charge again.

"No, we need to lay him on his back," Thomas instructed and moved to turn the sheriff around. This caused Peter to snap back to his regular self.

"Like hell you are Thomas. Why did you bring him here? He's got a home you know," he moved to block Thomas. "I built this table from scratch and I'm not going to let it get soaked with his blood."

"He's not breathing well, I don't want to block his throat. Besides, this man is your friend, are you going to let him die for the sake of your table?"

The only sound in the room was their labored breathing. Peter seemed to be considering both arguments with the speed of a lame mule. Mary was working in the kitchen, heating up some water to cleanse the sheriff's wounds.

"Fine, put him up here but if he survives this he's going to be the one building me a new table." Peter took up the Sheriff's arm and they turned him. With a single lift they got him up on the table.

In the faint light of the window the Sheriff looked pale. His breath reeked of Tequila and came only in faint gasps now.

Thomas squatted down next to the table, the blood returning into his muscles making him feel alive again. He watched as Peter collapsed into a chair, rolling his head from shoulder to shoulder before pausing with his head cocked to his left shoulder.

"What happened to his finger?" Peter asked plainly.

Thomas looked to Mary and then over to Peter. He didn't want to say anything, he wanted a moment to catch his breath. With Mary standing there he didn't want to talk about the scene at the tree.

"Mary, I'll watch the kettle, can you go take care of your horse?" Thomas asked. He knew what he'd seen out there, knew what he'd tried to hide from her eyes, he didn't want to have to explain it now.

"Okay, can I use your corral?" she asked, taking a moment to wipe her hands on the small apron she wore.

"Yeah, feel free to use anything you need. I'll cover it," Thomas responded, motioning to Peter not to object. No sooner was the door closed than Peter was out of his seat grabbing Thomas by the shoulders.

"Did the girls out at that ranch do this to him? Is that where you were last night? I'll start up a posse so fast..." his speech was cut short as Thomas knocked his arms free and pushed him back towards the chair.

"Look, you want some answers and I understand that. What I don't know is how you expect to get them when you're shouting in my face."

Peter collapsed back into the chair, his whole face looked sunburned with anger. Thomas gave him a moment to be sure that he wasn't going to react before continuing.

"I escorted two girls from the cemetery back to the ranch last night. It was late and I stayed in the bunkhouse with Samuel. On the way back she was getting the horse some exercise when we spotted the Sheriff hanging from a tree near the mission."

"So Sally didn't do this for revenge?" Peter asked, looking confused.

"Not that I know of. When we were cutting him down though there were a few things I noticed. Jonah's knife stuck in a sawhorse covered in blood was one of them."

Peter only nodded at the implications. They both knew that Jonah always kept his knife close, but what they didn't know was what the Sheriff had done.

"But why did he carve the word 'Coward' in his back? Why did he whittle the skin of the man's finger?"

Thomas shook his head, "You act like I saw it happen, but I didn't. If we hadn't come along he would have died out there."

An idea occurred to Thomas then, something that might explain it. "We never saw Jonah after we dropped Patrick off at the cemetery, did we?"

Peter thought for a moment before shaking his head. Thomas nodded back to him and made his way towards the door.

"Where are you going? Aren't you going to take care of him?" Peter motioned to the man on the table. "You brought him here after all."

Thomas opened the door and then paused to answer, "He's your friend, start getting him cleaned up. Mary will be in to help once the horse is cared for. I should be back in a few minutes and might have an explanation for all of this."

With that he headed out the door and hurried down the street to the Sheriff's house. When they had dropped the coffin off to be buried, Jonah had mentioned that the Sheriff had promised him a special bottle of rum from his cabinet for the work. Booze was one of the few things that could motivate Jonah to work. The Sheriff had told them the story of bartering for it off of a trader when he came for blankets. It hadn't been cheap but he assured Jonah that the flavor was excellent.

Everyone had known that the bottle would be almost empty when it was offered. What if something had happened with it? They all knew that you didn't come between Jonah and his booze.

Stepping up to the door Thomas reached for the handle, only to find that it wasn't latched. He took a breath, then a second, hoping that it would give him the courage to step inside. Yet he didn't know where Jonah was. For all Thomas knew, Jonah was inside, drunk, and holding a loaded gun.

"Jonah, are you in there?" Thomas called into the room. He waited for a minute before cracking the door open with his toe. The hinges creaked in the frame as it swung inward, and Thomas waited for a response.

He looked up and down Main Street, watching to see if anyone was looking his way. Seeing no one he called inside, "Hello, is anyone in here?"

Silence answered him from the open door. Taking a deep breath he felt his chest loosen, this was a good sign. He felt confident now that he wasn't about to get shot. He knew where the Sheriff kept his drinks and he made his way quickly towards the cabinet. Trying the door he found it had been cracked open, the wood around the lock splintered.

"Oh man, that's not good," he said to himself. Once the cabinet was open he saw that the bottle was missing. His world seemed to spin around him, he felt certain that he was about to be very sick.

Thomas ran out the door and down the steps, feeling acid rising in the back of his throat. His friend had attacked the sheriff over a bottle of alcohol. He was as certain of that as he was certain that the sun had risen this morning. There would have to be a posse. Homes would be searched. Bloodshed was all but certain.

"Jonah, why the hell did you do this?" Thomas asked himself as he tried to keep himself from crying.

CHAPTER 11

Patch stepped into the Sheriff's home as the first light of dawn was rising above the horizon. It'd been a long night, and the revelations of the evening still rang fresh in his mind. The thought of Sally being with Sheriff Roberts, or any of the other men in the area, disgusted him. It wasn't that he was against frequenting a lady of the night, in the last fifty years it had been some of the only comfort he'd received, it was trying to resolve the information with what his experience had told him.

The Sally he'd known for the last two years hadn't been the kind of woman that concerned herself with men. She was almost a nun without a habit. Her main concern was with the education of the girls and the running of the farm. To think of her in any kind of a sexual way was foreign.

Meanwhile, the Sheriff's words as he talked about her rang in his ears, bringing images unbidden to his mind. Thoughts of him on top of Sally, of the acts that they might have done, paraded through his mind's eye. He shook his head and glanced around the room he'd entered. The dim sunlight filtered through the back windows, the muted light making the room barely passable. Patch's eyes scanned the table and desk in the room, bottles littering what little open space there was. The desk was the only place that looked like any care was given to it.

Walking over he began to look over the papers which were scattered around the top. While there weren't many of these, the faded rings left by the bottom of bottles made much of the writing unreadable.

"So there are Marshals coming through next month for an inspection," Patch said to himself as he moved the papers. Then something else caught his eye, and he held it up to the light.

"So they're looking to run a rail line through this area. Wouldn't that be convenient for everyone? It'd make it so trade would be even easier, and if someone were to control the..." his words drifted off as things began to come clear. The whole thing began to stink of conspiracy and secret dealings.

He could imagine the Sheriff locking people up who didn't agree to the trade terms that he set forth. Allowing the things which they had made to fall to ruin while those who paid him off were allowed use of the station. It wouldn't last long, as the railroad usually brought a whole new set of problems to town. But that peg seemed to fit more soundly into the hole than the thought of jealousy.

A new image came floating into Patch's head, this one not full of lurid images of raised legs and moans. Instead, a group of people playing cards in a smoke filled room crowded into his mind. That was where Sheriff Roberts, his deputy, Samuel, and the rest were when the idea formed.

Samuel had probably mentioned how well he'd be doing with Sally once the Railroad came to town. Sheriff Roberts had chided him that they weren't a couple and they all knew it. After all, the Sheriff had done things with her that'd make him blush.

As this unfolded, Patch began to look to the empty bottles wanting a drink himself. He knocked over a stack on the table and began to search more frantically as things continued.

The air around the table seemed to thicken with tension as the scene in his mind played out. Samuel's cards lay on the table now, and he seemed on the verge of kicking his chair out and leaving. The rest of them watched as the Sheriff grinned back at him. That's when he finally said the words that set this whole thing in motion.

"You know, if you could control that market then I'd happily offer you the protection you want," Sheriff Roberts says with a grin, still looking over his cards.

"I know I can get control, I just need something to make her scared. If we light a fire under her and show her that she does need some protection, that is exactly what you'll have." Samuel promises. Patch knew that Samuel liked to talk big, and then would become angry when he was proved wrong. This probably didn't help one bit.

Patch notices as he comes out of his day dream a small cabinet near the kitchen with an ornate lock on it. Without a second thought he grabs a knife from the desk and jams it into the space between the lock and the cabinet exterior before prying it open. Inside lay several bottles of liquor, each one different and at least half empty. Scooping up the first three, he makes his way upstairs as the scene in his head continues.

Patch took a long pull from one of the bottles as he made his way upstairs. He knew that he'd probably drain the three he had and then take a nap. Now he hoped that the Sheriff was dead. If he wasn't dead then he'd have to finish the job tonight. He'd have to kill everyone at that table in his mind. The deputy was dead, the sheriff might as well be. But Peter, Samuel, Jonas, and that kid that worked for Peter. Each of them would need to face the knife tonight before he could move on. Perhaps then, the grip that seemed to hold his feet firm would loosen.

He finished the third bottle as he lay on the sheriff's bed, basking in the warm fuzz that the alcohol provided. The scene was on it's third play through as he felt the warmth carry him off to sleep.

* * * * *

A squeaking hinge brought Patch to his senses again. It was the one he'd heard when he first came into the sheriff's house. Someone had come inside, and someone was here sticking their nose where it didn't belong.

He tried to gauge how much time had passed, but the light had barely changed at all. Patch could still feel the warmth of the alcohol coursing through his veins which confirmed that not much time had passed. Had someone seen him enter? Had they come to hunt him down, to string him up all over again?

"Hello, is anyone in there?" a voice called out. Patch froze, uncertain if he recognized the voice. The fact was, someone had come looking for him and had found him.

Listening carefully, he could hear someone moving downstairs.

The footfalls were slow, cautious, as though they knew they were being watched. Patch looked to his side and saw an empty bottle labeled Rum next to him. He didn't know where the sheriff kept his weapons, but he knew that the knife he'd seen was laying downstairs amongst the discarded papers of the desk.

"Idiot," he muttered under his breath. "That's the second knife you've left behind today. You need to get your wits about you or you'll be digging yourself out of another grave."

His voice came out a whisper, but he still felt like it was echoing off the rafters. He pulled himself to his feet and felt his equilibrium shift gently. What a horrible time to get drunk!

Still no footstep's came from the stairs, they all seemed confined to the room which he'd trashed possibly hours before. Patch drew himself up and cautiously made his way to the edge of the staircase. If this person did come up the stairs, he was going to be lying in ambush.

"Oh no, that's not good," he heard the voice mutter and then the man hurried outside into the street. Patch felt adrenaline kick, pushing the haze of the alcohol out of his system. They were coming in now, he'd wasted too much time and become complacent. He had to act. Now.

He threw open the sheriff's wardrobe and began to toss everything he could out onto the bed. Finally, he pulled out an old worn duster and a pair of pants. Those would have to do, he figured, as he made his way over to the window overlooking the alley.

Patch held the thick material of the duster up against the glass and pressed firmly against it. The small pane of glass in the bottom right corner was the first to crack and break out. He did the same to the other three as quickly as he could. The last thing he wanted was for them to find him here at the top of the stairs due to the sound of the broken glass.

As he broke out the cross piece of the window he felt a bit of relief that no one had come through the door. He began to climb through the window as a bell in the center of town began to toll. He recognized it all too well, it was used to call a posse or a town meeting. It would be echoed at the mission and before long, anyone who called this place home would be in town.

Patch realized that his luck was near its end now. The hunt was beginning, and he was the prey. Within the hour they'd be searching for him. He'd have to make certain that he wasn't found.

CHAPTER 12

Thomas watched as Mary dabbed the cloth against Sheriff Roberts' lips to keep his mouth moist. He'd been running a fever for the past few hours and they were hoping that it wouldn't kill him.

"I think he's getting hotter," Mary said as she put the rag back in the bucket. "I can feel the heat through the cloth. I don't know if he'll last much longer."

That had been the consensus from when the fever had started. The posse was gathered together to form a plan when it had started. The Sheriff had been struggling to sit up the entire time the posse was there. As they were about to commence the search they had heard his voice in the background.

"Patch... Patch is..." and the rest of the words fell away into incoherent muttering. With this he slid from the table and onto the floor.

Several men had run over. Once the fever was discovered, it had been decided that someone should stay here and care for him as the others searched. So Thomas and Mary sat nearby, listening to the labored breathing.

"I hope he stays with us a little while longer. I want him to see justice after what was done to him," Thomas said. Mary nodded and brought the rag up again, mopping the Sheriff's brow.

A laugh sputtered from the Sheriff's lips, and for a moment Thomas was certain that he'd heard him say, "There is no justice."

He looked over to Mary. "Did you hear that? It sounded like he said..."

His words were cutoff as Sheriff Roberts pulled himself upright.

"Sir, you really should lay down. You're not well at all, and you're runnin..." Mary stated as she tried to pull him down.

"No!" Sheriff Roberts shouted, cutting her sentence short. "You don't know what you're hunting. He was dead, I know he was dead."

Thomas stood up and put his hands on one side of the man. He knew that at any moment he might lose consciousness and fall from the table. Mary took the other side and tried to coax him to lay back down.

"Sheriff, you're delirious," she started but he continued on.

"You don't believe me, I'll swear it!" he shouted as he fought the two of them. "I saw that look in his eyes as he questioned me. It was the same look as when he was laughing up there, dangling from the end of the rope."

Thomas could feel Mary still trying to coax the sheriff down, but something he said made Thomas pause. He'd been there, by the edge of the gallows as Patrick had kicked and swung on the rope. There had been a fire in his eyes as he had laughed, as though Satan himself was staring through them. A small shudder ran through his body as the laugh echoed through his head.

"Mary," Thomas interrupted. "We need to hear him out. If something happens to him..."

Mary paused before nodding in agreement, then stated "We'll listen, but he needs to lay down. I don't want to have to pick him back up off the floor again."

They both watched for a moment, uncertain if the sheriff was going to agree. Then with a nod, he allowed them to help him lay back down.

"I was drinking in my home last night, not wanting to go out to the bar. I knew Jonah should have been coming down to get the money and the bottle I promised him." He paused, then turned his head to Mary. "Could you bring me a cup of water to sip at?"

She stood and walked to the bucket, stopped to pick up a tin cup from the shelf, then she brought everything back.

"Well, I heard a knock at the door and assumed it was Jonah coming to collect. But when I opened the door it was that devil standing there grinning." At this point the sheriff stopped and took the offered water. Rolling onto his side he drank the cup once and refilled it before setting it on the table next to him.

"Now, I didn't know what to think, plus my mind was addled with the drink, so the next thing I know he has knocked me over the head and I woke up tied in a tree."

Mary and Thomas both looked at one another, both imagining the scene that they had found this morning. She shook her head and walked away, not wanting to hear any more. Thomas felt that, for the first time, perhaps he wasn't delusional. Perhaps there was some truth to the man's ramblings.

He'd seen the gaping wound in Patrick's chest. He'd touched the blood soaked material of Patrick's pants. He knew that he hadn't been breathing.

Then he remembered something that had been dismissed by Peter that night. When they'd gone to pick up the body he was certain that it had breathed on him. Was it possible that it wasn't crazy?

The sheriff had continued recanting his tale, but now neither of them were listening. Thomas felt a sudden need to go take a look at the grave that he'd only glanced at last night.

"Mary, last night did you see anything at Patrick's grave that was out of the ordinary?" Thomas said. The sheriff stopped mid-sentence and looked at her. Only then did he realize who she was.

"Where am I?" Sheriff Roberts asked aloud to both of them.

Thomas answered while Mary was contemplating the question.

"You're at Peter's house in town, lying on his table. Mary and her horse helped bring you here. We have a posse out searching for Jonah because of what he did. Now you're telling us something different."

"There was one thing," Mary stated once Thomas was done speaking. "The shovels were lying behind a pile of dirt that was still there. You probably didn't see it from the ground but from horseback I could see them."

Thomas knew Jonah was often drunk, but he knew better than to leave a good tool out in the weather. He was a drunk, not a lazy drunk. Plus he hadn't seen Tim that day either. Tim was always lazing around town in the shade. He hadn't come in with the rest of the posse. No one had seemed to notice.

"Were there two shovels there?" he asked to confirm with her. She only nodded at this. The sheriff turned his head and, after a momentary loss of balance, steadied himself on the table. Mary hurried over and helped steady him, then took a wet rag and placed it on the sheriff's head again.

"You're beginning to see it now," Sheriff Roberts said, looking at Thomas. "You think that if you went up to that grave and started digging, you'd find two bodies."

Inside Thomas felt torn. He wanted to head out of the house and start digging, but if what the sheriff said was true, then there was a killer on the loose. What did he know for certain?

Thomas began to review what he knew of the situation. He knew that Patrick had died and had been in the coffin. He'd nailed that top on himself, though without enough nails to make it really secure. His friend Jonah was missing, as was Tim, and someone had used Jonah's knife to cut up the sheriff. Sheriff Roberts said that it was Patrick, yet everything else seemed to point to Jonah.

"Can you prove to me that your eyes weren't deceiving you in the dark last night Sheriff?" Thomas asked.

The sheriff sipped his water and nodded to him. "I'm sure that my eyes were sound. But if you don't trust me, then at least let's head out and warn Sally. You can steer the horse and can bring me back if there is nothing."

"Why would we need to warn Sally?" Mary asked, looking concerned at the mention of her home.

"That is what Patrick was asking me about. He was wondering about Sally and Samuel's history. I figure if he was willing to torture me to get information, then imagine what he'd do to her," Sheriff Roberts grinned as he said this, though Mary wasn't able to see it.

He sipped more of the water, and seemed to be a less dizzy.

"We can't leave Patrick to go out there if it's really him. What if he does something to Sally... or Samuel," Mary stated, dropping the rag back into the bucket.

Thomas hadn't considered the farm hands in all of this. He wouldn't hurt the girls would he? That's why he'd killed the deputy after all.

"No, if it's Patrick, then we'd be safer staying away from the girls. He'll protect them, but I don't know how he'd like the man he tortured showing up. He might kill him on sight."

Sheriff Roberts slid himself off the table and then braced as he almost fell over.

"Sit back down Sheriff," Mary called to him and moved over to help him back down.

"No, I've sat for far too long. If you aren't going with me, then I'll go by myself." Sheriff Roberts then moved over to the chair by the door.

"Sheriff," Thomas called. "You can't go out there by yourself. I'll go with you."

"What about me? Am I supposed to sit here and take care of this place while put yourselves into a dangerous situation?" Mary asked placing herself between Thomas and the door.

"I don't know if we are riding into danger, Mary, but someone needs to let the posse know where the sheriff's gone when they check in. Besides, I'd feel bad about putting you in danger." Thomas tried to step around but felt her grip his arm firmly.

"Look, I know you're trying to be brave, but Patrick wouldn't hurt me and we both know it. Besides, the only horse out there is the one that belongs to Sally. If I don't show up with it than she may think you stole it. You wouldn't want to be thought of as a horse thief, so you're staying here."

The sheriff chuckled at this, before adding his own thoughts. "She does have a good point. I'll make you a deputy for now. You keep looking for Jonah like you believe. If you're right, you'll be rewarded. If I'm right, then I might need backup. After all, how do you kill a dead man?"

This thought sent a chill down his spine. Perhaps he would be safer here. Yet in the back of his mind, he felt a little voice calling him a coward for sending a woman in his place.

"Can you at least take a gun with you?" Thomas asked Sheriff Roberts.

"That's the plan, I was going to stagger over to my house and fetch one now while she readies the horse." Sheriff Roberts stood for a moment before falling back into the chair. "Perhaps you can help me get over there, then to the corral."

Thomas pulled the sheriff's arm around him and was surprised at how much cooler he felt already. While the plan wasn't the one he would have chosen, it felt nice to be doing something.

CHAPTER 13

The sunlight glared through the window and onto the bed, shining directly into Sally's eyes. She felt groggy and wanted nothing more than to fall back to sleep. Every time she inhaled it felt like her rib cage was going to crack. The muscles were tight, and she thought that the bones might be creaking, deciding whether to break or not. She tried to remember what had happened, but nothing came to her. Other things took priority in her mind at the moment, like the crick in her neck, and her sore shoulders and wrists.

The shoulders were the first indicator that something was wrong. Her shoulders rarely ever hurt. For them to hurt her while she was still in her bed was even more odd. Then she remembered snippets from the fight downstairs, the one where she'd taken a shotgun butt to the stomach. She had collapsed to the floor and blacked out, but then what? How had she come to be lying in her bed instead of in a ball on the floor below? None of this made any sense to her until she tried to move her arms, hoping to get the blood flowing. Her head whipped from side to side and she could see that she had been tied to the headboard of her bed.

Frantically her mind tried to figure out a way to out of this. She scanned the room, noting only in passing how happy she was that she was still wearing at least a shift.

On her nightstand lay her comb and the small mirror she used for her hair. Though there was nothing within her reach she could use to cut through the rope. She flexed her arms, hoping there might be some give in the rope, but instead found nothing wanted to move.

"Damn," she cursed to herself quietly. Sitting in the room and running through options, she could hear voices outside the window. It sounded like the girls were out washing wool. At least they were doing okay, but where had they been this morning?

She remembered calling out to Mary, remembered that she hadn't answered. In that moment she wanted to scream at the girl, to ask her where she'd been.

What good would it have done? It was her own fault that she was here, and nothing she could do would change it.

Her eyes glanced around the room again, noting that the window was closed, as was the door. He'd probably locked it too, another barricade between her and those who might help her. She knew that shouting would do no good, and neither would trying to wriggle free. That would leave her out of breath and likely in more pain than when she had started. So, instead, she sat and stewed in the mess that she'd made for herself.

Almost an hour had passed before anything changed, her fingers had gone numb and she was beginning to lose feeling in her hand. That was when she heard the key in the door. Someone was opening the lock.

Deep inside she felt a surge of adrenaline, at last someone was coming and could untie her. But she knew all too well that it was likely Samuel coming to check on her, to see if she'd changed her mind.

About what? She tried to remember, there was something the argument had been about? Had there been a frying pan? She remembered struggling, remembered trying to find the gun so she could shoot him. What had he been saying? His words were all still a blur despite several attempts to recall them.

"Sally, you're awake!" Emma called from the door. She carried a small washbasin and a pitcher full of water.

"Emma, are you girls all right?" she asked quickly. There were a million questions she wanted to ask, but she knew that if she asked them she'd be out of breath and hurting again. Besides, Emma didn't do well when flooded with questions.

"Yeah, why wouldn't we be all right? We're cleaning the wool like you asked us to. Samuel told us about you collapsing and said you needed rest," her eyes looked confused but innocent. That was something that Emma had always lacked, the sense of guile needed to tell convincing lies.

"Well, I'm feeling much better. Could you untie me so I can go talk to Samuel?" she asked hopefully. She didn't know what he had said but she was certain that he'd covered his bases. She wanted to find him, preferably asleep, while she carried a rather large kitchen knife.

Emma took the rag from the wash basin and then poured some water out of the pitcher. After wringing out the rag in the basin she brought it over and sat on the bed next to Sally. "I was told not to untie ya," she stated calmly before placing the cloth on her head.

"What? Did Samuel tell you that? Did he tell you not to untie me?" she felt herself getting frantic as the cool rag was dabbed across her face. While it did feel nice, it didn't help the situation at all.

"Yeah, we were worried when we came in to find you collapsed on the floor. Samuel said you had been shouting and angry. Then after, you just collapsed," Emma stood up as she finished. Taking the cloth back to the basin and rinsing it.

"That doesn't explain anything," Sally called back. Her voice was almost to the breaking point of being a yell. None of this was helping at all.

"Well, your fever has gone down, I'll tell him. Hopefully you'll be able to come down and have dinner with us," Emma said and then left the room. She left the washbasin on the dresser and closed the door behind her. Then, after a brief pause, there was the sound of a key in the lock and she knew that she wouldn't be getting any help from there.

She could feel her pulse in her neck now, knowing that at any moment Samuel would come through the door. Despite knowing how much it would hurt, she began to pull at the bindings even more. The rope slid as she moved, cutting into her skin, burning it as she fought. It took all her focus not to scream as she moved, her ribs still bruised, her arms now feeling like they were on fire.

"So, you finally decided to wake up?" Samuel asked from the door. She'd been so focused on the pain that she hadn't heard the key in the lock.

"Let me go you ass!" she heard the words as a growl, escaping her lips before they'd even registered in her head.

"That's no way to talk to the man who is helping you through this trying time," he said, and closed the door behind him. Then she watched as he inserted the key, locked the door, and turned back to her. "Emma said the fever had broke, but I don't know if the delusions have gone away quite yet."

She scowled back at him, glimpsing the game that he was playing. All he needed to do was move her out of the way for a few days, and the girls would answer to him like they did to her. Plus, the sickness made it so that he could lock her up for delusions whenever it was convenient. A part of her hoped that the girls weren't so gullible. She knew that Mary would see through it, but the rest of the girls were younger and much more innocent. They hadn't been taken advantage of before, like she had, and so they trusted easily.

Samuel sat down at the end of the bed, just out of reach of her feet, and grinned. "I'm sorry Miss Sally, but we want the best for you. If your delusions get out of hand they might cause you more harm, or worse, you might harm one of the girls."

"You know I'd never hurt them. I've given my life over to taking care of them. To training all of these girls so they have some kind of skills in the world. I don't want them to have to lie on their backs to earn a living like I did. They all deserve better."

She watched as he only nodded at her, letting her say everything that she needed to say. He didn't make a move to interrupt her or to challenge anything she said.

"Aren't you going to say something, you no good pile of shit?" she spat the words at him, and still he smiled. The room went quiet then, her waiting for a response and him sitting there silent. At least a minute passed before he finally spoke again.

"I'm sorry Sally, but it sounds like you're still a bit under the weather. I'll come back in the morning to see if you need anything. Perhaps by then you'll be able to keep some water down, or some food," he grinned at this.

Again the adrenaline rose and she pulled against the ropes. She coiled her legs underneath her and tried to get some slack; she had to do something to get to him. Yet as she kicked and tried to move towards him, he stood up and moved over to the wash basin. He took the rag and then walked over to her, the rag still dripping.

He began to wring out the water over her chest, the moisture of it making the shift she was wearing transparent. "You know Sally, you really shouldn't work yourself up like this. If something bad were to happen to you then I'd be left with this place. Is that what you really want?"

The cold water against her body made the fabric feel clammy. Already the moisture on her skin made the air feel cooler. He dipped the rag in the water and brought it back, soaking her again.

"You know, at this time of season you have to watch out for the cold. Those nights are liable to make you rather sick if you're out in them. Of course, you know that," he said wringing it over her again, and then going back for the basin and picking up the pitcher.

"You won't do this Samuel, I thought you said you loved me." The edge was gone from her voice now. She could see all too well where this was headed, and the last thing that she wanted was to lay shivering through the night.

"Oh, I do love you Sally. But you don't seem willing to love me back unless there is some threat involved. It's a great way to stay alive, but that's not the kind of relationship that I want. If you can honestly love me back, then maybe there is hope. Otherwise, I'm taking over and will find someone new," he punctuated this by throwing the remnants of the water on her, soaking her to the bone.

She screamed in shock, and then began to spit out the water which had splashed into her mouth.

"Now Sally, I'm sorry that you don't want to drink any of the water I offered. Let me open this window a little bit to help you dry out. Besides, a little fresh air will do you good."

As she blinked the water from her eyes she saw that he was already around the end of the bed and making his way towards the window. She had been out enough in the last few evenings to know that the frost was almost here. Perhaps tonight it would be cold enough to freeze what little they had left in the garden.

"No, please don't open it, whatever you want I'll do it," she began to cry.

"Well, I'll go ahead and open it for now, and then I'll check on you later tonight. Then we'll see if you're still feeling lovey-dovey. Perhaps you can even give me a bit of what is owed," he winked as he said this, and then lifted the window open a couple of inches.

Voices sounded downstairs, followed by shrieks from the girls in the kitchen. Samuel stood frozen, staring at something outside of the window. Sally wanted out of the bed, wanted to look around and see what was happening. Something was scaring her girls downstairs.

A snippet of her and Samuel's earlier conversation came to her then, bringing to her a bolt of realization. She could hear his voice now, talking about the Sheriff.

"The sheriff would turn a blind eye as long as he got what he wanted. Mostly some of the money and his choice of the girls from time to time."

She renewed her struggle against the ropes, her own screams joining those of the girls. All their voices were frightened; hers was shouting profanities at Samuel to let her go. She needed to be there, needed to defend her little ones like a mamma bear defended her cubs, but she'd been trapped. As the realization set in she collapsed, resigning herself to her fate.

Footsteps sounded on the steps, and then on the landing. Samuel made his way over to the door now, the look on his face as perplexed as she felt. What did he have to be confused about? Had his buddies shown up early? Were the girls showing more fight than they were supposed to?

She watched as he placed the key back into the lock and turned it. Then, gripping the handle, he began to turn it, cautiously, opening it enough to peek out of.

A heavy thud came from the door as it flew open, hitting Samuel solidly in the shoulder and throwing him backwards. From the doorway came a voice, one that Sally thought she had heard for the last time days before.

The evening light made it difficult to see clearly, but she was certain it was him. He stepped through the door and into the room, his features becoming clear in the fading sunlight. Around his neck was the burn from a rope, but there were no other signs of trauma.

"There you are Samuel," he said with a scowl. Patch picked Samuel up and walked him over to the partially open window. With one hand he held Samuel aloft, while his other lifted the window open to its full height. "Give me one reason why I shouldn't kill you right now."

Travis Coleman

CHAPTER 14

Patch stared at Samuel as he waited for an answer. The request had been simple, but the man blubbered and fussed instead of answering.

"Any time you are ready Samuel," he said, chiding the man. He could see Sally trying to come to grips with it. When he got a minute he'd have to go over and untie her, but for now he had more important things to deal with.

"You're dead. You were shot in the chest," Samuel blurted, his eyes still wide in shock.

Patch rolled his eyes and picked him up a little higher off the floor. Then looked out the window to see that his scarecrow was staring up at him.

In the middle of the pasture, tied to a stake with a noose around his neck, was Jacob. Patch knew that he was merely unconscious, but from up here he really looked dead. He grinned as he realized that a bit of burlap and some straw would make his scarecrow look complete.

"Patrick, he's got a knife," Sally yelled from the bed. Patch spun in time to see not a knife, but a pair of shears stabbing down towards his shoulder. He pulled back, trying to dodge the blow. Unfortunately he still held Samuel by the shirt front. Instead of dodging the blade completely, he changed where it hit, missing the shoulder and embedding itself into the meat of his bicep. As Samuel tried to pull the shears, Patch's left arm knocked his hands free.

Patch felt his own grip relax, a clatter coming from where Samuel had just hit the floor. Already he was scrambling to his feet, trying to put some space between himself and where Patch stood. Patch took the moment to grab the shears and rip them from his arm, an inch of the blade crimson with blood. While he looked at the blades he could hear Samuel climbing to his feet.

Swinging his leg, Patch kicked at Samuel's knee, hoping that it would throw him off balance. Instead, Samuel jumped backwards and into the wardrobe that stood in the corner. Patch tried to follow up, bringing the shears around to stab, but Samuel dodged again. This time he rolled back around the wardrobe and threw the door open as a barricade between the two of them.

"You haven't answered my question Samuel. If you don't, then you'll definitely die. If you do, then you might live longer before you die," Patch muttered as he tried to maneuver between the door and Samuel's wild punches.

"Get away from me you demon," Samuel cried. "You're the Devil incarnate, back from hell. Be gone Satan!"

Patch began to laugh, the outburst catching Samuel off guard. Never had he been called the Devil before, but he guessed there was a first time for everything. Besides, usually when he'd been called evil it was by someone who felt guilty.

"I know what you did, that's why your friend the sheriff spent the night hanging in a tree. That's why the deputy was buried and I was hanged."

Instead of trying to get around the door, Patch dropped the shears and grabbed it. He pulled the door towards him, the wood of the wardrobe crunching as the hinges overextended and ripped free. Behind the door he could see that Samuel had paled, knowing that Patch knew everything.

"You..." Samuel stammered. "You can't be..."

"But I thought I was the Devil. If I can be that, then I can be anything...including an angel of vengeance," as he finished he lunged and grabbed Samuel with both hands, this time backing up towards the window.

Samuel struggled, kicking and screaming the entire way. Yet as he moved closer to the window, Samuel's hands instead tried to hold him away from the wall.

"You can't throw me out. I've still got things..." Samuel began before being interrupted.

"So did I. I was about to leave town when this little plan of yours started. Had you waited, I wouldn't be your problem."

"But... but..." Samuel stammered, but Patch knew he was playing for time. Samuel was kicking at him and trying to move them away from the window. Patch was prepared this time, and forced him backwards. Samuel resisted moving his feet so Patch did the next best thing, bending him over backwards and forcing his head through the open window.

"No, I'm sorry for what I did. I was just jealous," the words came flowing from Samuel's mouth now.

Patch didn't wait, instead he grabbed the heavy window and pulled it down hard, pinning Samuel's neck. He turned, saw the shears lying on the floor, and spun to pick them up. The window began to move upwards as Samuel tried to get enough room to release his head. Patch had expected it.

He pivoted, the shears held high, and with all the weight he could muster he brought them down into the wooden frame of the window. There was a creaking from the frame as Samuel continued to push, but the effort was futile. Samuel was trapped, and Patch could get some answers.

"Samuel, please tell me why you didn't stick up for me at the trial," Patch stated. He paced just beyond the reach of Samuel's kicking legs. Behind him he could hear voices coming from downstairs, yet Sally said nothing. Perhaps she wanted to hear this as much as he did.

"I told Sheriff Roberts that I wouldn't," he began. Patch didn't wait, instead he stepped forward and gripped Samuel's right arm. He pulled it out at an angle and kicked into the armpit. There was a crunch and a pop, punctuated with a scream.

"You wanted to see justice done, well here is justice." Patch yelled over the screaming. He then walked around to the other arm and took the wrist. "That last one was for what you did to Emma."

He grabbed the left arm and kicked again. Both arms now hung at unnatural angles, the screaming from Samuel intensified at this new pain.

"That one was for our dear Miss Sally here. I don't know what you were going to do, but she deserves better."

He turned, walked over to Sally, and began untying the rope around her wrists. She was frozen, watching Samuel squirm with eyes wide and her jaw slack.

"It's okay Sally, he's getting his justice now," Patch stated and removed the rope from her first wrist. He watched as she slipped away to the other side of the bed and began to loosen the other rope. She didn't say anything, but he understood.

At the window the cries had faded, they were now moans, which he felt were appropriate.

"Go downstairs Sally, keep the girls safe while I deal with him," he said as she finished untying the other rope. She pulled the damp blanket from the bed and wrapped it around herself.

"Patrick, the things he was going to do," she began. He waved her off and motioned back towards the door.

"He's got devils in hell in store for him. He'll be joining them shortly," Patch smiled. That was when he noticed that she wasn't looking at him as a friend or employer any more. Instead she had a look on her face of abject fright, as though she was seeing him for the first time.

She walked to the doorway, looking back over the scene. He saw her eye the wrecked wardrobe, her soaked bed, and then Samuel flailing in the window.

"Please don't," she asked. The look in her eyes told him that she didn't believe it would change things. She knew all too well that Samuel was getting everything that he had asked for. Patch shook his head. Without another word she turned and left the room.

"At least she'll be able to sleep knowing that she tried," he said to himself quietly as he turned back to Samuel.

Patch could see that he was beginning to black out from the pain and the impaired wind pipe. At least that meant that he wouldn't be awake for the final blow. It was a small mercy, yet he knew that the revenge wouldn't be any less satisfying.

Pulling the shears from the window he opened them up and examined them. Then he cut away the shirt from Samuel's chest, one side of the shears stained crimson from the remnants of his own blood. He watched the chest rise and fall in a steady rhythm as he closed the shears.

Patch thought about saying a few words, thought about telling him what he thought of the plan, but he could feel the blood lust coursing through his veins. Adrenaline flooded his veins in a rush which came only in those moments before the kill. He felt like a coiled snake ready to strike.

His hand swung out, not at Samuel, but towards the wardrobe, building momentum. Then he brought the hand back, underhand, jabbing up through the stomach cavity and piercing the heart. Blood gushed from the wound, the body cavity filling to capacity. The deed was done, and it was time to go.

He left the room and made his way across the landing. His feet felt lighter, as though the chains which had bound him here had been released. With his revenge satisfied, he felt torn on whether he wanted to be here or not. He did feel bad about what had happened, but he didn't want to be here to sift through the aftermath.

He leaned on the banister and looked down the stairs. No one was below him, and he knew that the girls had probably all fled out the back door and into the barn. That was fine though, the last thing he wanted to deal with was more people. For the time being he felt drained and needed to make some decisions.

"Patrick," Sally called from downstairs. He knew he should answer, and began to make his way down to her. He really hoped that she wasn't upset at what he'd done to Samuel. She'd left him to do it though, wasn't that enough of an indicator?

"I'm here. Samuel isn't with us anymore," he said as he made his way down the stairs. There wasn't any response as he walked. He didn't care, he realized that she might also be in shock after all of the violence which had transpired. As he rounded the corner, it wasn't Sally's voice which greeted him.

"Patch, you should have finished the job," Sheriff Roberts said. He stood in the doorway of the kitchen, holding Sally in front of him as a human shield. Over her shoulder he held his pistol pressed against her temple.

Patch froze, Sheriff Roberts wasn't something which he'd planned on. He realized that, despite trying to figure out what to do now, he'd been planning on walking out that door. Now he felt his blood run cold as he saw her held there.

"Sheriff, I've got the revenge that I needed. I'm leaving. Let her go," Patch stated. He could see that the Sheriff didn't move. He could see that the kitchen door was still open, and feel the cool wind blowing in.

"You were supposed to be dead. That was the sentence, and I'm here to make sure that it's carried out," the Sheriff stated as he pulled the hammer back.

"Don't you dare shoot her! She's innocent of all this. The only reason she's involved is because of Samuel's little plan. You let her go and we'll settle this like men," Patch held his hands out to his side. He hoped that the Sheriff wouldn't take him as threat. He didn't want to hurt her any more than he already had.

"I'm not gonna shoot her, I'm gonna shoot you," he said and whipped the gun towards him. The trigger pulled and Patch felt pain shoot through his chest. Looking down, he saw blood running from his right lung as the hammer clicked into place a second time.

"Patrick!" Sally yelled and threw her elbow back into the Sheriff's gut. The second shot went wide, splitting the wood above the front door. Sheriff Roberts threw her forward into Patch and took aim for a third shot. His breathing was heavy, and Patch could see that he looked to be shaking visibly.

"You know that's not going to stop me," he said as he caught Sally. He spun around to put her behind him, and then stood up straight. He moved toward the Sheriff, his hands at his side, blood still oozing from his lung. He wished he'd brought the shears down, without a weapon this would be more difficult, but he'd killed with his bare hands before.

"Stay back Patch," Sheriff Roberts called, punctuating his statement with another shot. A hole appeared in his chest, still on the same side. He could feel his right lung filling with blood as he pressed on.

"It'll take more than that to stop me," he grabbed the Sheriff's gun arm and threw it out to the side. It collided with the door jam causing him to drop the weapon. Patch could feel the heat coming from the Sheriff's skin and knew that he was burning himself out. Likely some kind of infection had taken hold from when he'd been cut. He needed a new lung, but the last thing he wanted to give himself was a terminal infection.

The struggle continued, the Sheriff trying to get down to grab the gun. Patch tried to push him into the kitchen to where he could find a weapon.

It took almost a minute before Patch finally got the leverage that he needed. He dropped beneath the sheriff and pushed him back into the room. His shoulder thrusting into the Sheriff's gut and knocking him back onto the table.

There was a crash as the table broke under the Sheriff's weight. Patch stepped into the room to see a skillet full of onions and potatoes on the stove, far past cooked and beginning to smolder. He grabbed an apron, which was lying next to the stove, and lifted the skillet.

As the Sheriff Roberts climbed to his feet, he brought the pan around with a heavy thud. The man fell to the floor screaming, his hands clutching the scorched skin on his face. Patch dropped the skillet and picked up the knife sitting on the counter next to the onion scraps. He turned and thrust it into the Sheriff's lung, mirroring his own injury. Patch watched as the Sheriff quit screaming, the blood ebbing from the wound. Then everything fell silent, he turned and stepped through the kitchen door only to be greeted with the sound of a single gunshot.

Falling to his knees, Patch stared at his chest. This time the shot had been true, and he'd been shot through the heart for the second time this week. He fell to the floor, the lack of oxygen becoming more apparent as his blood drained out of him.

"Patrick, no. Oh, Patrick," Sally exclaimed, the gun dropping to the floor. "I meant to shoot Sheriff Roberts if he came out, but I was so nervous..."

He wanted to talk, but his breathing was becoming more difficult. He knew that he'd die tonight, perhaps this time he wouldn't come back. Tears began to fall on his cheeks as Sally cried over him. She was trying to talk, but there were no real words to say, so instead she wept.

"It's... okay," he uttered to her as best his breath would allow. He didn't want her to be there, he wanted her to leave, to run far away. But it wouldn't happen, she'd committed to him now. She pulled his head onto her lap and began to run her fingers through his hair.

"Patrick, I never wanted to hurt you. You were the one man in this town I think I could have loved," she sobbed. She picked up the blanket which had fallen from her shoulders and draped it over him.

Patch watched her as she cried, uncertain of what he would do. He hadn't felt so loved since he'd been a child. His life had been a string of chaotic events, never allowing himself time to get close to anyone. But here it was, he'd finally found someone who would love him, and he'd fought to save her life without even thinking of it.

That wasn't the love he'd been told about. He'd always been told as a child that if you loved someone, you'd give everything for them to be happy.

"I only wish there was something I could do, something to make your suffering a little more bearable."

He motioned for her to come closer, before uttering the words, "A... kiss..."

She nodded and bent down to press her lips against his. Her arm gripping his shoulder as he reached around and pulled her tight. The kiss only lasted a moment before they separated.

Patch looked up at her, her face beautiful in the low light. "Thank you."

"You're welcome Patrick, you're..." but her words were cut off by his hand piercing into her abdomen, the nails sharp and carving through her flesh. Her eyes went wide, her mouth trying to find something to say, but nothing came out.

His own chest began to open then, to welcome the new parts they would be receiving. He didn't smile, this hadn't been what he wanted. The instinct to survive was too strong inside of him. She'd offered to do something to make the suffering end, and he'd taken advantage of it. It was time to go. He needed to move on, this wasn't where he was supposed to be buried. Not yet...

EPILOGUE

Thomas sat outside the barn while Mary calmed the girls inside. He knew that at any moment someone would be coming out of the house. It could be Samuel, perhaps it'd be the Sheriff. He hoped it would be the Sheriff.

He could hear sobs from some of the girls behind him, but to his surprise Emma sat next to him. Seeing Patrick coming into the house hadn't bothered her. She seemed to think he was more of a guardian angel than a criminal on the loose. Thomas didn't know what to think of him, but knowing that someone who he'd help bury was still walking around was unsettling.

"It'll be okay Thomas," she said to him. Her reassurance was comforting, though he wished that her presence would be more comforting to him. He wished that Mary were here, and hoped that things wouldn't change between the two of them after all was said and done.

He'd grown to like her in the last day and a half, and it wasn't common for him to get along with women. Even now, he could hear her singing a lullaby inside to the gathered girls, and the sound of it relaxed his mind.

The door opened and out stepped a man, through the darkness he couldn't be certain of who it was. The man looked around before walking towards the barn. As he made his way over, Thomas realized that it wasn't the Sheriff. "Stop right there," Thomas yelled, though he was a little surprised to hear the words coming out of his own mouth. When they'd found Daisy in the corral the Sheriff had made him a deputy. Now he wore a gun hanging at his side, but if Patrick was walking across the yard he stood no chance of surviving a confrontation.

"Or what," Patch asked as he kept walking.

That was the question. What was he going to do? Before he could think of anything, Emma ran across the yard.

"Patrick," she shouted and threw her arms around his waist. Thomas watched as he paused and hugged her back.

"Hello Emma, is this man treating you okay?" he asked.

"Yeah, he's a good guy. I think Mary likes him," she said.

Thomas felt his cheeks burn slightly and hoped that she was right. The man didn't make any move towards a weapon, but instead took Emma's hand and led her back to the barn. When they got there he picked her up and set her on a saw horse.

"What happened in there?" Thomas found himself asking. It was the only thing he could ask. He felt certain that everyone else inside was dead. He didn't really want to know how it had happened either. Besides, if the Sheriff and Samuel couldn't stop this man, then how could he?

"There was fighting, Samuel had attacked and killed Sally. Then the sheriff showed up and Samuel stabbed him. I caught Samuel by surprise upstairs, pinned him in the window and stabbed him with his shears. Now I'm leaving, there is nothing for me here," he said it all with a straight face.

"No, you can't leave us Patrick!" Emma cried and climbed off the saw horse. She ran back to him and tried to hug his legs again. Tears streamed down her cheeks from the news of Sally's death. "You can't leave us all alone. Not without Miss Sally."

From inside of the barn the door opened, letting some light spill out. Thomas could now see that Patch was covered in blood, two bullet holes in his chest and one in his stomach. He didn't know how Patrick was still standing.

"No Emma, you stay with him. I'm going to take one of the horses, and I need to leave," Patch told her. "It won't be peaceful around here until I do."

Thomas knew they hadn't unsaddled the horses which they had ridden out, so they'd be ready to go. While he wanted to send him away with Peter's horse, he knew that would result in a beating. He realized while thinking this that he was the last remaining deputy, which usually that meant that he would assume the job of the sheriff. The worry of beatings evaporated and he felt a smile come to his face.

"I have a horse for you to take. She is over there, her name is Daisy," he said and then turned to see who had opened the door. He could see Mary's head peeking out through the crack in the door. None of the other girls were able to see, and he was sure she was keeping them well away from the doors.

"Thank you," Patrick stated. "Now don't think about shooting me in the back, or I'll do to you worse than I did to Samuel or the Deputy."

Thomas only nodded and watched him walk away. For all the blood on his shirt, he was surprised at how easily the man mounted the horse. Within minutes he was riding away into the darkness. Once Patch was only a shadow on the horizon Mary stepped out of the door.

"What are we going to do now? I heard about Sally and the rest," she asked Thomas. Emma was still crying, sitting collapsed in the dirt while tears streamed down her cheeks.

"I really don't know, but I believe I'm the sheriff now. I think we need to take some time and make certain that this kind of thing doesn't happen again," he said, and then stepped over to Emma. He helped her to her feet and led them into the barn. Tomorrow they'd need to arrange for burials, Peter would be upset about the extra work but Thomas didn't care. He'd have Mary to take over the farm here, perhaps with Jacob's help if he was still alive. He glanced to the form still tied to a post in the middle of the yard. He would come out for him a little later.

He'd need to take the time to think tonight. After tonight there would be no time at all. As the barn door closed, so did his worries about everything outside of it.

ABOUT THE AUTHOR

Travis Coleman lives in Logan, Utah, with his wife and two children. He spends his spare time writing stories, playing RPG's, and reading as many books as he can find time for.

For Author news follow him on:
Twitter: @TravColeman

or on his blog at
http://travcoleman.blogspot.com

www.ingramcontent.com/pod-product-compliance
Lightning Source LLC
Chambersburg PA
CBHW020634130626
46552CB00003B/1221